# The Scandal of Rose

## A GILDED AGE NOVELLA

JOANNA SHUPE

# *Prologue*

Rose

*February, 1896*

HE LOVED TASTING the two of us together.

As Moore eased down the length of my body this morning, that familiar wicked gleam in his eye, I could hardly wait. He had just pulled out, his orgasm still seeping from my center, and I trembled with unfulfilled lust. I was delirious for him.

My breath caught in my lungs when his tongue met my pussy, his growl vibrating in my very soul. Then his tongue slid over me, swirling, dancing. Worshiping me with his mouth. He seemed dedicated to his task, lost in the act, and I wasn't complaining. Moore knew exactly what I preferred after three months, and each lick and suck sent sparks up my spine. Tension coiled inside my belly, my muscles growing taut, and I gripped his hair in one fist to hold him closer.

Shutting my eyes, I chased the high and rocked my hips. Moore was an expert at this. He once said he'd choose licking me over fucking me any day. I was glad we never had to choose because I loved it all.

I swore I'd never become a rich man's mistress. I traveled that path before and it ended in heartache. Therefore, I resolved to keep my liaisons casual and sleep with a man only once, no matter what.

But then I met Moore.

And there was every possibility that I'd fallen in love with him.

Indeed, a cliché for a mistress falling in love with her protector. But Moore was different. He was a good man, a *caring* man who looked after me like no one ever had. We talked about anything and everything and I made him laugh. Mostly, I wanted to bring him happiness, as he did for me.

He lifted his head. "Are you mine?"

I gave him the words in my heart. "I'm yours, Moore. Yours alone."

He hummed deep in his chest, then sucked on my clitoris once more. "Oh, *god.*" I clutched his hair in my fist. "God, yes. Darling, don't stop!"

Then I was soaring. Pleasure flooded my veins and I started convulsing, shaking with the force of the orgasm he'd wrenched from my body. It went on and on, his tongue never letting up as I continued to come, nonsensical words falling from my lips and into the yacht's lavish cabin.

When I finally collapsed onto the mattress, he eased up and gave my intimate flesh the sweetest of kisses. "Was that good?" he asked with a crooked half-smile, already knowing the answer.

"Come here." I held my arms out until he crawled higher and stretched beside me. "You know it was good." I kissed his jaw. "Any better and I'd incinerate."

He pressed his lips to mine and gave me a deep kiss. I tasted myself, but also the mint from the fancy tooth polish he used. He paid a pharmacist to import it from France, because only the best would do for Mr. Alfred Moore Emerson III.

We broke apart, but didn't pull away. His mouth hovered over mine, our warm breath mingling. "Christ, I already want you again."

Moore liked when I used crude words. Women in his world never did, so I made it a point to say them whenever possible. "Fuck me again, Moore."

As if on cue, he lunged for my mouth, his kiss urgent and hungry.

His palm cupped my breast and squeezed. Eventually, he eased back. "Damn it, woman. I do have to leave this cabin at some point today. There's a mountain of work awaiting me."

"The work can wait." I nipped his lower lip with my teeth. "I haven't seen you much this week. Stay and make it up to me."

I knew I sounded needy, something I swore I'd never be with a man again. After all, I'd pleaded once to another and it had done little good. Humiliation followed, an entire community casting me out.

Yet I'd missed Moore these past few days. Thank goodness he'd taken me on a sail where it was just the two of us surrounded by miles of cold ocean water.

His blue eyes were soft with affection and sincerity. "My darling Rose, you know there is nowhere I'd rather be than here with you."

"Prove it."

"Rather thought I just did," he quipped, tipping his head toward my lower half.

"You're impossible." Smiling, I smoothed the sweaty hair off his forehead. "Let me remove my womb veil. Then I'll return."

I started to rise, but he caught my arm. "Wait. I need to talk to you."

The serious manner in which Moore spoke the words gave me pause. He was normally relaxed with me, a generous lover who was so different from the broody man I first met.

I ran the underside of my foot along his bare calf. "What is it, darling?"

"Something has arisen this week. I'm trying to manage it, but I wanted you to hear the news from me instead of the newspapers."

The happy warm feeling disappeared as dread settled in my stomach. "Are you ill? Is it something with your business?"

"Nothing like that." He exhaled heavily and stared at the wall. "It's a nuisance, really. And it won't affect what we have."

"Is it the town house? I told you I didn't need you to buy it." Yet Moore had insisted, saying it offered better privacy than a hotel and the money was a drop in the bucket to him. But if he was facing financial hardship, I would easily give this up. I didn't need his money—I just needed *him*.

"You're keeping the house." His voice was stern, unyielding. Exactly like the powerful tycoon he was. "And I don't care to rehash that argument."

"Then please, tell me what is going on."

"I am engaged."

# Part One

# One

Rose

*Six weeks earlier*
*Union Square Theater*

ANOTHER HALF-FULL HOUSE. This show was awful—an over-the-top, self-important farce. Audiences had steadily dwindled since opening night.

Which was how I noticed *him*. The man in the box on the right side of the stage.

This wasn't his first appearance in the theater. He'd been attending for *weeks*, every night, alone. An older gentleman, perhaps mid-thirties, well dressed. Handsome. I could feel his eyes track me as I performed, an intense dark stare that sent heat arrowing through me. It was as if I could taste his interest, his desire, from across the stage.

At first I thought I was wrong, that he watched all the actresses as intently. I quickly learned this wasn't so. Any night when my understudy performed in my place, I was told the mysterious stranger stood up and walked out.

Yet he hadn't approached me. No flowers or notes had arrived backstage, as was customary from admirers. Instead, he gifted me only with his remote attention night after night.

I became fascinated. Who was this swell? I asked the crew and my fellow actors, but no one knew his name, and he always left before I could seek him out.

Not tonight, I'd decided. *Tonight I will have answers.*

My skin buzzed with anticipation as the final curtain fell. Instead of participating in the bows as usual, I darted into the wings and toward the front of the theater. I hurried to the stage door, where the guard waited. Through labored breaths, I asked, "Did you see, Jimmy?"

"I did, Miss Rose." He propped the heavy metal door open for me. "That nice lacquer one right there."

I peeked out. Sure enough, a fancy black carriage waited at the curb. I handed Jimmy a coin. "Good work. Distract his driver, will you?"

"You'll land me in trouble, one of these days," he murmured, but stepped out onto the walk.

When Jimmy began arguing with the driver about blocking the street, I slipped outside, still in my costume. Very carefully, I opened the carriage door and eased inside. Ducking low, I closed the latch behind me and settled onto the velvet seat. Lord, it smelled nice here. Clean, with a hint of oak and cigar. A far cry from the stench of refuse and waste that lingered on the downtown streets.

Jimmy finished his fake argument and returned to the stage door. Now all I had to do was wait.

One thing about me? I was tenacious when I set my mind to a task. No matter how long it took I would sit here until the stranger returned. And I wouldn't give up until he told me his name and explained why he kept attending this show night after night.

Bodies trickled out from the theater doors. Was he wondering about my absence from the curtain call? Was he disappointed? I bit my lip, my blood humming as each portentous second ticked by.

The carriage door suddenly flew open.

A large figure filled the doorway, his face in shadow. He paused, fingers gripping the door, and I could feel him staring at me. Weighing his options.

"Hello." I patted the seat next to me. "Do come in, won't you?"

His lips twitched ever so slightly. Not looking away from me, he told his driver to stay put.

Then he removed his silk top hat and stepped up. Long legs folded as he arranged himself elegantly on the seat across from me, and I could see his features better now in the low light inside the carriage. Strands of silver threaded the dark hair at his temples, so a bit older than I'd first thought. He had a sharp jaw and high cheekbones, and a wide, arrogant mouth. There was something commanding about him, as if he belonged on the bow of an ironclad, waging a battle on enemy warships.

Still, I wasn't intimidated. I could wage war, as well.

He spoke first. "This explains your absence at the curtain call."

I batted my eyelashes dramatically. "Had you noticed? I am touched, sir."

A touch of color dotted his cheekbones. "Why are you here?"

Direct. I liked it. I folded my hands on my lap, which had the added effect of compressing my bosom. His eyes remained on my face, dash it. "I've come to ask why you are attending each of my performances."

"Perhaps I appreciate the theater."

"And I would call you a liar, sir."

"That's bold of you."

"Hardly, when I haven't a clue as to who you are."

A long second ticked by before he nodded once. "Alfred Moore Emerson III, at your service."

"Goodness, so many names," I murmured, my mind whirling. So, he was an Emerson. Nearly everyone on the island of Manhattan had heard of the family at some point. Like it or not, the richest and most powerful always received the most attention, and New Yorkers were obsessed with their version of royalty, the Knickerbockers. "I am Rose O'Donahue. But you already knew as much."

"Is that your given name, or a stage name?"

I could feel the hairs on the back of my neck stand up. I didn't like this question. Rose Doyle—the girl I left behind in Youngstown, Ohio—was no more. She had died years ago. "Are you attempting to annoy me?"

"As you have stowed away for an ambush, I do believe that shoe is on the other foot."

I didn't care for how he was turning this around on me, clearly deflecting. He struck me as a man used to having the upper hand in each situation. But I would not be cowed, not when I'd felt his gaze on me nearly every evening.

I leaned in slightly and lowered my voice to a husky rasp. "Mr. Emerson. You haven't missed a performance in three weeks, except for the ones I skipped. Were you hoping to gain my attention?"

"Don't be ridiculous," he snapped. Much too quickly, it was worth noting.

I couldn't keep from smirking. "I see."

"Miss O'Donahue, pray wipe that expression from your face. You are far too young for a man of my age."

Which meant he'd thought about it. Quite a lot.

Hmm. Who possessed the upper hand now?

"You may call me Rose . . . *Alfred*."

He swallowed hard, his throat working in the shadows of his collar. "Moore."

"I beg your pardon?"

"I prefer to be called Moore."

I nearly grinned. This was the most fun I'd had in ages. Normally, I performed and went straight home to a lonely apartment downtown. "How old are you, Moore?"

"I told you, too old. Now, remove yourself and let me be on my way."

So prickly. Was his age a sore subject, then? I shook my head. "Not until I receive answers."

He tapped his gloved fingers on the seat in an impatient rhythm. "Perhaps I am bedazzled by your abilities. You are regarded as one of the best actresses in the city."

"Are you? Bedazzled, I mean. You hardly seem the type."

If possible, he appeared even grumpier. "Meaning?"

"Meaning that a man born with a silver spoon in his mouth would be difficult to impress."

"I apologize if my presence has offended you," he said after a beat. "I will cease attending after tonight."

"No." I would wither in this awful production without Moore's attention on me. His regard kept me engaged in the role and made me feel alive. There had been admirers before now, but none this . . . intense.

He blinked twice. "No?"

"You haven't offended me, and there is no need to stop attending."

"I disagree. My curiosity in regards to you has been satisfied and there is no need to continue."

"Curiosity?"

His chin rose slightly, the proud bearing of his shoulders evident through his black evening coat. "Surely you must know."

"I don't, actually. A curiosity regarding my intelligence? The capacity to hold a conversation not first memorized on a page?"

"Miss O'Donahue. *Rose*." Moore cocked his head and frowned. "No one who watches you on that stage could ever doubt any of those things. You're remarkable."

I soaked in the complement and considered begging for more. Actors are such vain creatures. "Thank you. May I guess your age?"

His mouth curved and I could swear that amusement danced in the depths of his dark gaze. "Only if I may guess yours in return."

"Fair enough."

I pursed my lips and studied him. Since moving to New York four years ago, I hadn't paid much attention to the lobster set, which meant I really didn't know his family history. I could only judge by what I saw now, like the little lines creasing his forehead, framing his eyes. No lines bracketed his mouth, suggesting he didn't often smile. Evening stubble kissed his jaw, which, along with broad shoulders, spoke of manhood. "Forty."

Disappointment and irritation flashed over his face. "Thirty-eight," he said sharply.

I held up my palms. "I beg your pardon. Perhaps if I saw you smile, I might've shaved off one or two years."

"You are quite bold."

"I assume you mean that as a compliment, so thank you."

"Actually, I did not." He sounded amused, so I wasn't the least bit offended.

I shifted under the lamp to give him a better view of my features "Now, it's your turn to guess. How old do you think I am?"

"Twenty."

"Very good. I'll be twenty in six months' time."

"Christ," he said under his breath before dragging a hand over his face. "I should be tarred and feathered."

"For being attracted to me?" No use trying to hide it. We both knew it to be true.

"Yes—rather *no*. I am not attracted to you. You're practically a child."

If only he knew all the hardships I'd endured in my life. "I haven't been a child in a long time, Moore."

"Well, to me you are almost a child. Though I must say, you look older on stage."

"It's the cosmetics. Without them, I appear my age."

"Ah, that explains it."

We sat in silence for a minute. Was Moore searching for a mistress? If so, I needed to set him straight. Many actresses I knew had benefactors—men who paid for their lodgings and lifestyle in exchange for intimacies. I never judged them. This city was hard enough and everyone deserved a little help now and then. If not for a lucky break, my existence here might've turned out much differently.

Yet I wasn't interested in a benefactor. I had dreams of financial freedom, one that depended on no man. One that couldn't be taken away or leveraged. One that was all *mine*.

Only when I was financially secure would I choose a husband and move out to a big house in New Jersey or Connecticut. I'd grow flowers and have children and all the happiness in the world. This, however, was years away.

In the meantime, I enjoyed intimacies with a man, much in the way I enjoyed the attention I received while onstage. Both were brief, all-encompassing feverish endeavors that left me sweaty and drained, but in the very best way. Then it was over and I could relax with a good cup of tea, alone.

Unfortunately, there hadn't been a man in *months*. My last lover, a young man on break from his studies at Yale, fumbled through our encounter, leaving me unsatisfied and bored. The urge to try again hadn't occurred until now.

Moore, I was certain, would not fumble. Not even a little. I hadn't slept with a man in his late thirties before, but there was an air of arrogance around him, and I found it headier than any cologne. My gaze traveled down his chest and over his thick thighs. He looked athletic, fit. Certainly not the type to stay indoors and watch a ticker tape all day. He was probably insatiable . . . I licked my dry lips.

"Are you in search of a mistress?" I blurted. "If so, I hate to disappoint you. I don't sleep with a man more than once."

"You should go," he rushed out, his voice choked as he reached for the door handle. "I bid you goodnight, Miss O'Donahue." He eased the carriage door open, revealing us to the theater patrons lingering on the walk.

"There she is!" someone outside cried. "Rose! Miss O'Donahue!"

The crowd swelled near Moore's carriage and I decided to take pity on him. Theater fans could, on occasion, become rambunctious. But this was far from over.

Gathering my skirts, I slid closer to the door. "I'll see you tomorrow, Moore."

"You won't. Good luck in the rest of your run."

I threw him a challenging glance over my shoulder. "I will see you again. Mark my words." Then I climbed down to the walk and faced my admirers as they circled around me.

Moore's carriage didn't depart until I went inside the theater.

# Two

Moore

EXHAUSTION WEIGHED me down as I climbed the polished marble steps to my front door.

*I will see you again. Mark my words.*

I shouldn't have gone there tonight. Instead, I should've stayed far away from Fourteenth Street. Yet I'd craved another glimpse of Rose like a hop head seeking a hit of opium. Everything about her drew me in, from the ample curves I longed to explore, to her wide, lush mouth that promised wicked delights. This was no tightly corseted debutante who tried to blend into the wallpaper rather than be noticed. No, Rose O'Donahue bloomed under an audience's attention until you couldn't possibly look away.

And meeting her had tripled my fascination. She was witty and clever and far too bold. I liked it. A lot.

No wonder she was so popular.

None of this mattered, however. She was far too young, and I wouldn't sully the Emerson name again with a second scandal. One was enough to last a lifetime.

Distracted by thoughts of green eyes and red hair, I didn't notice my mother lurking in the hallway when I stepped inside.

"Goodness, there you are," a feminine voice said. "I've been worried about you."

I passed my coat and hat to Peters, our butler, with my thanks. Then I smoothed my hair and went over to greet my mother.

After my divorce I sold the home I'd purchased for my former wife and moved back to Fifth Avenue. God knew my mother had enough space, and living here meant that I could look after her. The scandal from the end of my marriage had caused my father's untimely death, and the shame and guilt haunted me daily. At least here I could ensure my mother's continued health while atoning for my mistakes.

"Good evening, mother." I kissed her cheek. "I didn't expect to find you up at this late hour."

"I was waiting to speak with you. Come into the library."

I was bone-tired, but denying her would appear churlish after she'd waited up for me. In the library, I poured myself a drink as she settled on the leather sofa. The room, with its scents of heavy leather-bound books and lemon polish, reminded me of my father. The two of us spent quite a lot of time here when I was young.

He'd prepared me well to take over Emerson Holdings, a business that has been in my family since the days of Hamilton and Madison. Every day I swam in numbers—the market, the gold standard, the price of commodities. I studied, invested, and managed to turn money into more money. I was good at it, though it often felt as if the responsibility consumed my life. As if happiness were a luxury afforded to everyone but me.

My former wife's parting words as I put her on a cross-continental were to call me the coldest man she'd ever met. No matter how hard I tried, I could not make my first marriage work. My wife's profound unhappiness could not be breached, and no amount of attention from me had ever brought about a common understanding between us.

I lowered myself into an armchair. "You seem agitated. I trust you are feeling well?"

"I'm perfectly fine. I keep telling you, stop worrying about me."

As if such a thing were possible. My father would be here holding her hand and kissing her cheek, if not for me. "Is something amiss, then?"

"Mr. Whitney-Dunn has paid a visit today."

A longtime friend of my father's, Whitney-Dunn was patriarch of a prominent Society family and had lost his wife a few years ago in a tragic boating accident. He also sat on the board of Emerson Holdings. "Oh? And what did he want?"

"To discuss the possibility of a marriage."

I choked on a mouthful of whiskey. The two of them? *Married?* I couldn't begin to comprehend it. "You can't be serious."

She arranged her skirts, avoiding my eyes. "Well, I was surprised, as well. I knew Gladys had debuted, of course, but I didn't think she had designs on our family."

I paused in the process of blotting drops of whiskey off my silk vest. "Wait, who is Gladys?"

My mother stared at me as if I were cracked. "The daughter. Whitney-Dunn's youngest. You remember her, don't you?"

"Can't place her. I'm double her age, if I recall."

"Not quite, but nearly. And you know those things don't matter as much as people think."

"Except to the bride, who'd no doubt prefer to marry someone not so ancient."

She waved her hand as if brushing my comments aside. "Let's not stray off topic. Whitney-Dunn would like for you to marry Gladys."

"No."

She pursed her lips together, the closest my mother ever got to a frown. "You don't even wish to consider it?"

I finished my drink and set the empty glass on the side table. "Hardly requires any serious consideration, as far as I'm concerned. Subject firmly closed." I edged forward in my chair, intending to rise. "Now, I'm exceedingly tired. May I escort you upstairs?"

"Wait a moment." She raised her palm. "I'm not finished. You were at the theater again tonight."

I held still, not liking the sudden change in this conversation. "Yes. What of it?"

"Off-Broadway is . . . seedy, Moore. It's unseemly of you to be downtown in those places, especially when we have a perfectly acceptable box at the Metropolitan Opera House."

But Rose wasn't at the opera house—not that I would ever see her again. I sipped my drink and tried to wash the bitterness from my mouth. "You sound snobbish."

"Call me a snob if you like, but I don't like you associating with those types of people."

"I enjoy the productions downtown," I lied. "And there is nothing seedy or unseemly about it."

"I'm told you attended alone."

Christ, the gossips in this town. Could a man not obsess these days without it being discussed over cucumber sandwiches up and down the avenue? "I still fail to see how this is a problem."

"Moore." She toyed with the three-strand pearl necklace hanging low around her neck. "We both know of your past. Your proclivities. Which is why I wish for you to marry again. It's time. Past time, really."

*Proclivities.*

All because I'd hired a chorus girl to lie in my divorce proceedings about an affair that never happened. While the tale had been the most expeditious path to granting Eugenia her freedom in New York, I sorely underestimated the city's appetite for gossip, the zeal with which the press would relish an Emerson's downfall. And the unholy scandal that followed had damaged my father's heart and sent him to an early grave.

I vowed then to live quietly, respectably. To dedicate myself to the family business and never give reason for anyone to malign the Emerson name again. And if I found the existence miserable, I had no one but myself to blame.

A promise I'd kept until recently, the night I spotted Rose O'Donahue.

Inhaling, I let it out slowly. "Mother, I am not marrying again."

She continued as if I hadn't spoken. "Miss Whitney-Dunn is the perfect choice. Good family, pretty enough. And you know how these things work. If you marry, then you may quietly carry on with whomever you like."

Carry on with an affair. Because that was what the city expected of me, an immoral adulterer.

I could feel an ache settling between my temples. My mother meant well, but this was a conversation I was unwilling to entertain. "My answer remains no." I rose and started for the door. "Now, if you'll excuse me, I am headed to bed."

"You must listen to reason, darling," she said as I crossed the room. "You've been dragging your feet, which is understandable, but the only way to repair the damage from the unpleasantness with Eugenia is to marry again."

Except there was no repairing the mess I'd caused. Marrying a second time wouldn't bring back my father. It wouldn't take away the reports of the trial, the newspaper headlines. The looks and whispers that followed me for the past eight years.

No, there was no taking any of it away.

As I reached the door, I said sternly, "I don't want to hear another word about marriage. Good night."

"Am I allowed to mention grandchildren, then? Because I would really like one or two of those before I'm gone. And I'd much prefer they were legitimate."

"If that is an attempt at humor, I'm not amused." Speculation of a baby had run rampant during the divorce proceedings, with every newspaperman on the East Coast wondering if the chorus girl was increasing with my child.

"Moore," my mother said with a sigh. "You're too serious. A wife would bring you joy, not to mention look after you. I'm concerned you are too stuck in the past. What happens after I'm no longer here?"

A cold sense of dread seeped into my veins. Was this about her health? I turned and studied her carefully, but there were no outward signs of illness. "That's twice you've mentioned your death. What aren't you telling me?"

"Nothing." She waved her hand. "I'm perfectly well. And it is a parent's role to worry over their offspring, not the other way around."

Except when said offspring was me. I would never stop worrying about her. It was my burden, my penance. If I'd insisted Eugenia travel to Reno, ignoring her aversion to long train rides, to obtain a quiet divorce, the scandal would've died down after a week or two. My father might've lived. He would be here to coddle and protect my mother, as he'd done throughout their marriage.

"There's no cause for worry," I told her. "And let us both agree not to raise the subject of marriage or grandchildren, legitimate or otherwise, ever again."

She frowned, but didn't argue. Eager to put this conversation behind me, I left to climb the stairs, hating myself with every step. I was a fool. Why had I attended Rose's show night after night? Deep down I knew my repeated appearance there would draw unwanted attention and dredge up comments from the past. Except I hadn't been able to stop myself.

*I don't sleep with a man more than once.*

God help me, that statement had been like waving a red flag in front of a bull. The all-consuming need to disprove it, to sink into her wet heat for as long as I desired, to give her orgasms under every phase of the blasted moon, had nearly choked me in the carriage.

Little wonder my mother was worried.

It was times like this when I hated being an Emerson, hated living in this city. Watched everywhere I went, my whereabouts reported on as if I were a lad instead of thirty-eight years of age.

But there was no help for it, which was why I needed to stay away from Rose. She was too young, the risk too great.

The problem was that I almost wanted her badly enough not to care.

# Three

Moore

*One week later*

I STRODE PURPOSELY across the old oak floor, passing desks full of busy workers. Two of my assistants trailed behind and peppered me with questions along the way. Emerson Holdings catered to most of the Fifth Avenue families, our fingerprints all over the wealth accumulated in this city. The Knickerbockers entrusted me with their meager stockpiles of cash that I turned into massive holdings for generations to come. Exactly as my father had.

As I approached my office, Mrs. Williams, my secretary, shot to her feet, hands wringing. Never had I seen her so flustered. The woman served as a Union spy in '64, for god's sake.

I stopped by her desk. "What is it?"

"Sir, there is a woman. Inside your office. I tried to stop her . . . ."

A woman? My mother would rather travel to Brooklyn than come here. And no one else would dare enter my office without my approval. "Who is it?"

"She wouldn't give me her name, Mr. Emerson. But some of the boys in the office seemed to recognize her, I think. They were whis-pering something fierce as she walked over from the elevator."

Irritation pulled at my muscles. "I'll see to it. Thank you, Mrs. Williams. In the meantime, we have several cables to send." I motioned to my assistants and instructed them to confer with my secretary.

Then I threw open my office door, ready to battle—and stopped in my tracks.

*Rose.*

Rose O'Donahue, in my office. Here, at Emerson Holdings. Sitting boldly in a chair, every bit as beautiful as I remembered.

Fuck.

Her glorious red hair was tucked under a simple hat, her wide smile a siren's call to each filthy thought in my head. No cosmetics, so her pale fresh skin practically glowed with youth. Forbidden, practically a babe, yet I couldn't tear my eyes off her.

Ignoring the jolt of heat that settled in my groin, I closed the door behind me. Thoughts of turning the lock went through my head, but the indignity of it wasn't to be considered. This was not that sort of meeting.

"Miss O'Donahue," I said mildly, attempting to quell the riot in my bloodstream. "I believe I made myself clear during our last exchange."

"Hello, Moore. You haven't been at the theater all week. I grew alarmed."

I strode toward my desk and sat behind it, the expanse of wood a much-needed fortification. "As you can see, I am perfectly well. You may return to your business."

"I don't think so," was her answer as she removed her gloves. Then she reached to the floor and produced a wicker basket. "Have you eaten? I'm famished."

Eaten? Basket? What in the goddamned hell?

I tapped my fingers on the century-old oak desk that once belonged to my great-great-grandfather. "Miss O'Donahue, I insist that you leave. This is highly inappropriate."

"I knew you would say as much." She reached inside the basket and produced a neatly wrapped parcel, which she set on the desk. Then she rummaged in the recesses of the wicker again. "You see, I feel it is only fair to linger at your place of business, considering that you lingered at mine for over three weeks."

Was she daft? "It's hardly the same. Yours was a public performance for which I purchased a ticket."

Another parcel. Then a tea cup. "This is a publicly traded company, for which I have recently purchased one share of stock. I am now your shareholder, Mr. Alfred Moore Emerson III. Is this how you treat your shareholders?"

"If they arrived unannounced? I'd have them tossed."

"Then toss me." She peeked at me through her long lashes and placed another tea cup on my desk. "But I won't go quietly."

"This is blackmail." I scowled at her. "And unless you have a kettle and gas stove in there, we won't be having tea together."

With a dramatic sweep of her arm, she produced a bottle of wine. "I much prefer wine, don't you?"

Drinking wine? With a famous young actress in the middle of the day? I could only imagine what my staff would say, if it were discovered. Her presence here was bad enough. "No wine. And I don't have time for visits."

"That is probably true," she said as she uncorked the wine. "You see, I've learned quite a bit about you in seven days' time."

A pit of uneasiness bloomed in my stomach. No doubt she'd heard the worst, as the disgrace attached to my name never quite dissipated. "Good. Then you know all the reasons you should leave."

"Do you think your past scares me?"

"It should."

"Your wife divorced you for infidelity. That is hardly first-degree murder, Moore."

"In some circles of Fifth Avenue, murder would be far more acceptable," I said dryly.

She poured a splash of red wine into each tea cup. "Were you unfaithful?"

I hardly ever talked about my failed marriage. It was a subject best avoided for my peace of mind. Which didn't explain why I said, "No, but—"

I closed my mouth.

When I didn't finish, Rose pushed a tea cup of wine across the desk to me. "But a divorce cannot be granted in New York without a claim of infidelity on one spouse's part. So you fell on that particular sword. Have I gotten it right?"

Yes, she had.

Needing to wash the surprise and embarrassment from my mouth, I reached for the tea cup. After a long swallow of wine, I stared down my nose at her. "Why are you here, Rose?"

She cradled her tea cup in both hands. "Curiosity. After our meeting in the carriage, I couldn't help but wonder about you."As she sipped, she kept her green eyes fixed on me across the porcelain rim in a clear challenge. "Aren't you curious, Moore?"

The meaning behind her words couldn't be clearer, and my heart began pounding an unsteady rhythm.

God, yes, I was curious. *Too* curious.

But I was also too old.

There was a group of men, all members of a certain gentlemen's club, who engaged in improper activities with young women, girls really, and I found it utterly deplorable. Though Rose was nineteen, not fifteen or sixteen, our circumstances weren't much different, considering I was almost twenty years her senior.

"It hardly matters," I forced out. "I never intended to pursue a friendship with you. I was content to watch you from afar, in my seat. Nothing more."

"And yet here we are, sharing a drink together in your office."

I set my tea cup on the desk with a decisive thump. "You've had your fun. It's time to go."

"Interesting choice of words, Moore. Because I hear that is the one thing sorely lacking in your life: *fun*."

I bristled. Did she believe me to be sexless? A eunuch? That I stalked the aisles of Broadway theaters because I couldn't find a woman elsewhere?

If so, she needed to be disillusioned immediately. And perhaps if I spoke plainly enough, crudely enough, then the truth would scare her into leaving.

I sat forward, my voice low and harsh. "Do you think I'm incapable of finding a woman? That I'm not presented with a willing pussy every time I walk around this city? If so, then let me assure you that within minutes I can step outside these doors and bury my cock inside a woman. I hardly need a girl half my age offering me a pity fuck to bolster my confidence."

She said nothing, leaving me to assume my words had the desired effect in shocking her.

But then her lips parted and her breathing picked up. There was a slight tremble to her hands and her eyes were considerably darker. She shifted in her chair.

Oh, Christ. Had I *aroused* her?

It seemed incomprehensible. Improbable. Inconceivable. My thoughts scrambled, and the words capable of cleaning up such a debacle caught in my throat.

Breaking our stare, Rose set her tea cup on the desk very carefully. Then she stood up—and my muscles relaxed. Excellent. She was leaving, then.

I nearly exhaled in relief. At least, I assumed this feeling coursing through me was relief. Because anything else was unacceptable.

Except she didn't walk in the direction of the door.

Instead, she wound her way around the desk and came toward me, causing every part of me to tighten again. What was she about? I couldn't move, my body frozen in place, the air growing thick with each of her steps. A surge of longing tightened every muscle in my body as she drew near.

*Please, no. I am not strong enough for this.*

She made her way to my side, the gentle rustle of skirts increasing in volume until they stopped altogether. I was hyper-aware of her proximity and the simple task of breathing eluded me, while my skin crawled with a hunger I barely understood. I was a watch spring, pulled taut, my insides spinning and twisting with both dread and anticipation.

One hand came to rest on my desk and the other slid onto the back of my chair. She leaned in and the sweet smell of her enveloped me— roses, naturally. I held the scent in my lungs, and my fingers dug into the armrests of my chair as if I were a sailor clinging to a rope in a typhoon. I was afraid to let go of the wood for fear I would do something idiotic.

She angled closer and I could feel her warm breath on my cheek. "It would not be pity, Mr. Emerson," she whispered in my ear. "Not even close."

I was out of my chair without even realizing it, lunging at her. My hands captured her face and I held her there, our eyes locked together. "Why are you doing this?" I rasped, one last valiant attempt at sanity.

"Because I haven't been so drawn to a man before. I have to know what it would be like." And she eased forward to close the distance between us, her mouth sealing to mine.

The first touch of her lips was awkward, but magnificent. Soft yet firm, the plump edges brushed over mine, moving gently, and I savored each sweep and press. I savored her like a drunk with his last sip of wine, memorizing every detail.

Unable to help myself, I began kissing her back. There was only pure instinct, the need to get as close to her as possible. She moaned into my mouth, and I'd never heard a sweeter sound in all my days. When her fingers slid into my hair, clutching, I wrapped one arm around her back, securing her.

Yet it wasn't enough.

I pushed her lips wide with my tongue, invading to find hers. She was wet and warm and—*Christ*—so eager that it turned my cock stiff as stone. There was no shyness, no hesitation. No concern for the fact that we were in my office in the middle of the day, almost twenty years between us. There were only panting breaths and tiny gasps as our tongues dueled for dominance.

For a man accustomed to numbers, I had no idea how many seconds or minutes passed. I only knew I wasn't ready for this to end. Flares of desire raced through my blood, my balls growing heavy with my need for her. I wanted to lick her creamy skin, bite the heavy mounds of her breasts. I longed to undress her and discover all of her soft secrets right here with little thought to the consequences.

Madness. Utter madness.

*Immoral.*

*Adulterer.*

*Scoundrel.*

I broke off and tried to catch my breath, as well as my rapidly dwindling sanity. Despite what the newspapers said about me during the divorce proceedings, I did possess scruples.

But then I saw the lust-drunk expression on Rose's face, her bee-stung lips. Green eyes that pleaded for me to keep going. And I paused, indecision gnawing at me.

Damn it. *Pull yourself together, man.*

"Moore?" she asked, confused, and the sound of my name in her low, husky tone was my undoing.

I was lost. Defenseless to her charms because I wanted her too badly. So many nights I'd watched her, wondered about her, about *us.* Wondered what I would do if I ever had her alone.

And now I did.

I wasn't about to squander this opportunity.

My fingers pressed into her skin, holding her tight. "Do you truly wish to know what it would be like?"

Her eyes cut to the room around us. "Here?"

"It's your one chance, Rose."

"Then absolutely. Yes," she breathed, no hesitation whatsoever.

"Clever girl. Now, climb onto my desk," I ordered. "And lift your skirts."

# Four

Rose

**WAS I DOING THIS?**

We were near strangers, yet I felt as though I'd been aware of him for a long time, watching me in the theater. And I'd learned quite a bit about Alfred Moore Emerson III in the past few days, thanks to a friend at the *New York World*.

Born to a high society family, Moore took over the business when his father died eight years ago. There had been a nasty public divorce, one of the first New York divorce cases involving someone of Moore's status. Mrs. Alfred Moore Emerson III claimed adultery on Moore's part, and a woman alleging to be his lover testified in court about the proclivities enjoyed by Moore on a regular basis. This had led to salacious articles in the newspapers for almost half a year.

After that, he hadn't remarried. In fact, after the divorce he'd lived quietly, almost respectfully. With no hint of a trouble whatsoever.

But I knew a little something about scandals, having lived through one myself back in Ohio. Maybe he and I weren't so dissimilar after all.

And after that kiss? My body was humming, ready for more.

So yes, it appeared I was doing this.

I moved the half-full tea cup on his desk and pushed the papers out of the way. Then I climbed up onto the wood and settled my skirts. Moore didn't assist me, but he was close. His big body looming before me, the heat jumping between us nearly singed my skin.

I wasn't lying when I said I hadn't experienced such a strong, instantaneous reaction to a man before. After just one kiss from Moore, my blood hummed. The tips of my breasts pressed shamelessly against my corset, begging for attention, while slickness coated the insides of my thighs. I wanted to find out what it was about this man that turned me into a mindless, lust-filled creature.

When I looked up at him, the wicked gleam in his dark gaze caused a shiver to race through me. Daylight streamed through the windows and reflected off the silver threads at his temple. His jaw was pure determination. "Skirts, Rose."

I grabbed the layers of silk and cotton and began lifting them higher, revealing my legs. Were we going to screw right now in his office? I wasn't altogether opposed to the idea, but he might want to lock the door first. "Aren't you worried someone will walk in?"

"No one would dare." He dragged his gaze down my half-clothed legs, an agonizingly slow sweep. "The benefit of being a surly bastard most of the time."

Biting my lip, I toyed with the folds of my skirts. "So what now, Mr. Emerson?"

He lowered himself into his chair and scooted closer. Yet he didn't touch me, his hands firmly on the armrests. "I want to see your pussy."

The crude word from such an elegant man caused me to shiver. "Do you always talk so lewdly to ladies?"

"Only to ladies aroused by lewd talk. Ladies like *you*."

So he'd noticed that earlier, had he? I hadn't tried to hide it, exactly, but I hadn't expected him to read me so well. I was an actress, after all.

"Skirts, Rose," he ordered. "Show me."

Perhaps I should've felt awkward, but having his rapt attention gave me confidence. I lifted my skirts and slowly eased my knees apart. He sat perfectly still, murmuring, "That's it, keep going. You're soaked, aren't you? I can see you've ruined your poor drawers."

I spread myself open, my hot center revealed to him. His nostrils flared and his chest heaved. "Oh, you are a mess. Look at that beautifully swollen flesh. Would you like for me to stroke it?"

I was nodding before he even finished the question. I did this at least three or four times a week myself, more so when I needed to relax. "Please, Mr. Emerson."

His eyes flicked to mine. "A proper and respectful girl deserves a reward, don't you think?"

A rush of desire flooded every part of me. I didn't need to fake my reaction or pretend with him, as I had with other men in the past. Moore cut past all my defenses to give me exactly what I craved. Hmm, perhaps I did the same for him? I whispered, "Yes, sir. I do."

With a growl, he angled forward, his big hands pushing my thighs impossibly wider. "Lie back. Let me taste you."

Taste me? *Oh*. I tried to hide my surprise as I eased onto the surface of the desk. In my experience, most men didn't bother with activities that were solely for me. They skipped right to the part where their cock was involved.

I was eager to see what Moore could do. Fifth Avenue tycoons weren't known for their generosity, after all.

A hot, wet stripe of his tongue went through my folds, across my clitoris, and euphoria rippled through me. But there wasn't time to recover because he did it again. And again. Always with flick in the precise spot where I craved him the most.

"Christ, you are delicious," he mumbled between licks. "I could devour your pussy for days."

I wished he would. This was leagues better than any attempt in the past. This was a goddamn revelation.

I glanced down at where he rested between my legs, his dark head bent, eyes closed as he returned his mouth to my flesh. This time he focused his efforts on my clitoris—and I nearly jolted off the desk. The pleasure was not to be believed. "*Oh, god!*"

He rubbed his palms on my thighs. "Relax, sweet girl." He kissed the nubbin of flesh. "I will give you what you need."

I couldn't move, couldn't object—nor did I want to once he set himself to his task. He sucked and licked, his tongue relentless, and I could feel my insides coiling, the pleasure gathering in my toes. At some point he draped one of my legs over his shoulder, and I dug my boot heel into his back, trying to bring him closer. I was sweating and gasping, my head thrashing on the ledgers and papers underneath me—a reminder that we were in his office, during the day, when anyone might enter.

Only a naughty, shameless tart would allow this.

It rushed over me then, as if a dam burst. I bit my lip to keep from shouting, and then I was climaxing, my limbs trembling uncontrollably. My womb convulsed in sweet pulses and sparkles exploded in my bloodstream, yet he didn't let up. "Yes, yes, yes," I whispered. "Oh, god."

Seconds—or, perhaps it was minutes?—later I returned to myself. My skin grew sensitive, so I wriggled when Moore gave me another lick. "Please, no more."

He rested his forehead on my mound, his shoulders heaving as we both tried to catch our breath. Dazed, I threaded my fingers through his soft hair. At any second he would rise up and shove himself inside me, pumping until he climaxed. I wanted to enjoy this blissful, selfish moment a little longer.

"Thank you," he murmured. My hand fell off his head as he straightened. He flicked my skirts over my legs, covering me. "I'll see you off in a hansom."

His expression was etched in granite, his movements abrupt. Was he so anxious to be rid of me, then? But when he stood to help me sit up, I quickly recognized the problem.

A very *large* problem.

His trousers were tented with an erection that could not be missed. I smiled, pleased he'd been so aroused by my body. And it put us on even ground, because *this* was a problem I could solve. This particular act, I knew.

I allowed him to assist me to my feet. But when he tried to step back, I chased, keeping close as I placed my hands on his chest. "Won't you have a seat, Mr. Emerson?" I blinked innocently up at him, yet he wouldn't meet my eye.

"Rose, I must return to my duties here. We've had our fun. Now it's time for me to see you off."

"But I can't possibly leave you in such a state."

I started to drag my hand to his groin, but he grabbed my wrist, preventing me. "Don't."

"Why not?" I stared up at him, confused. Men never said no to this. "I don't understand. You don't wish to finish in my mouth?"

A shudder went through him. Then he inhaled deeply and let it out slowly. His fingers released my wrist in order to sweep a rogue curl behind my ear, his big body relaxing slightly. "What does a sweet girl like you know about sucking a man's cock?"

"I know that you'll like it. I'll like it, as well." And I did. Even on my knees I felt powerful, in control of everything around me. A goddess. The act wasn't taken; instead it was given. A gift of nothing but pleasure, exactly as he'd just bestowed on me.

I could tell he was wavering, so I pressed closer and nipped his jaw with my teeth. "Wouldn't you like to see my lips sliding over your shaft? Or my tongue bathing your crown and making it wet?"

"*Jesus Christ*," he hissed softly. "When you use those words, I can barely resist you."

"Then don't resist. You won't be able to concentrate for the rest of the day if I leave now." I ran one fingertip down the center of his abdomen, then lower, and even lower until I reached the bulge in the cloth. I touched him lightly, teasing. "Please, Mr. Emerson?"

He drew in a deep breath, then took a step back. I could see his defenses going back up, the powerful man of business in place once again. I knew I'd lost.

This was confirmed when he said, "I'll escort you to the curb. We'll act polite, but that's all. No one can suspect anything untoward took place here today."

Disappointment pressed on my shoulders, but I wouldn't beg. I had my pride, and it was far more fun when men were begging for *me*. Not the other way around.

I shrugged. "Suit yourself. But I think everyone will have their suspicions when they spot *that*." I pointed to his groin.

He dragged a hand down his face. "Give it a moment. When it calms down I'll walk you out."

I didn't require an escort. Though it was sweet of him to offer, I'd been looking after myself for a long time. I pinned my hat, then packed up my wicker basket and lifted it off the floor. "I'm hardly a debutante, Moore. I can see myself off. Besides, would you walk one of your shareholders to a hansom? I think not."

The scowl he wore was fierce. "You and I both know you aren't a shareholder."

"Yes, but *they* do not." I waved my hand toward his office, which had been filled with young men toiling away at their desks. "It arouses suspicion if you escort me like a beau."

I decided it was pointless to argue with him. And I was at an advantage. I could leave the room, while he could not. "Goodbye, Moore."

"Wait—"

But it was too late. I was already at the door. "The performance is at seven o'clock sharp. Don't be late."

"I won't be there," he said, almost angrily. "What happened here today cannot be repeated, Rose. I've endured enough unwanted attention for a lifetime. I am not looking to keep a mistress, especially one so famous."

"Famous!" A wide grin burst free on my face before I could prevent it. "What a lovely piece of flattery. Well done, Moore."

"I am serious," he snapped. "Today is the last time we will see one another."

He was trying to convince himself, obviously. I didn't believe it, not after the way he'd kissed me, with such desperation and hunger. Not after the way he'd licked my center so feverishly. Not witnessing the erection in his trousers that had yet to dissipate. "I'm certain you are wrong. But don't worry, I'm not angling to be your mistress. As I said, never the same man twice."

Repeat encounters required a level of trust in a partner, and I didn't trust anyone other than myself. I'd believed in passion and promises once, only to be spectacularly burned. I would never fall victim to a pretty face or flowery words ever again. I would marry, but it would be my choice, years from now when I was ready to move out of the city and give up acting.

"Does this not count, then?" He tilted his chin toward the desk.

"No. This was a . . . an overture. Neither of us removed our clothing. Your intimate parts never met with my intimate parts."

The edges of his lips twitched like he might be fighting a laugh. Putting his hands on his hips, Moore stared at his feet. "Rose, that is utterly ridiculous."

"My rules, Mr. Emerson. They only need to make sense to me. Until tonight!" I let myself out of his office and pretended to ignore all the eyes on me as I strode to the elevator.

# Five

Rose

**HE DIDN'T SHOW** up that night.

Nor the next. Nor the four that followed.

Now I was riddled with doubt, wondering if I'd misjudged the situation. Or if I'd dreamed of the blistering attraction between us. Wasn't the man anxious to repeat what happened in his office? I was nearly crawling out of my skin from the memory. He'd taken such care and consideration with me, giving me an orgasm to shake the rafters.

I wanted it again.

The first three performances with Moore's usual box sitting empty were positively awful. I flubbed lines and missed cues. It was so bad that the director, after berating me for twenty minutes, threatened to recast my part. So I forced myself to concentrate and put the issue of Alfred Moore Emerson III aside, at least when I was on stage.

Today was a matinee performance, with cheaper ticket prices popular with students and Bohemians, which kept the high society types away. I tried to gather my enthusiasm. At least I could focus on my performance and not on the empty box, seeing as how Moore wouldn't be here.

Where was that blasted man?

By the time I left my dressing room, the piano player was well into the overture. I arrived backstage as the curtain went up and waited for my cue. The moment I stepped onto the stage my skin began to prickle. Something was different. There was an electric charge in the air, one I felt in my bones.

I quickly recited my opening lines, then looked up toward the box— and my breath caught. A large figure sat deep in the shadows, far away from the edge. But I knew.

*I knew.*

I bounced on my toes as giddiness bubbled up inside me. He'd returned. Moore hadn't been able to stay away, just as I predicted.

Over the next hour, I put all my effort into my role, as if I performed just for him. The audience laughed and cheered me on, but I was really trying to impress one person. I wanted his eyes on me at all times.

Finally, the curtain fell for intermission.

"You're quite the spark out there today," Flora, one of my co-stars, said as we left the stage. "I haven't seen you this animated in days."

I hid a grin. "Thank you."

"Any sign of your admirer?" Flora bumped my arm. "You know, the wealthy one."

I'd confessed a bit about Moore to Flora, when she asked me about my dark mood the other night. "Maybe."

"I knew it! Is he up in one of the boxes?"

"I think so. I'm going to find out during my break." I had a stretch of twenty minutes where I wasn't onstage in the second half—and I knew precisely how I planned to spend it.

Flora chuckled as she opened the door to her dressing room. "Just don't miss your cue, honey. The director will kill you."

I gave her a salute, then went into my dressing room. I freshened up, changed my costume, then waited for the show to restart. After my scene concluded, I could barely breathe as I edged into the wings. Anticipation twisted in my belly, pulling and tightening like vines, and I hurried toward the staircase leading up to the loge. An usher was posted at the bottom of the stairs and his eyebrows lifted dramatically at the sight of me. I put a finger to my lips and he nodded, pulling aside the curtain and allowing me to climb the steps.

Moore was *here*. In the middle of the day, instead of working. I didn't know why he'd come downtown this afternoon, but it didn't matter. I wasn't about to let this opportunity pass.

Nothing could've prevented me from seeking him out.

The corridor behind the boxes remained empty. Fancier theaters had salons behind the boxes, but we didn't. This meant I needed to be careful and stay out of the public view. I hunched over and slipped through the curtain to enter Moore's box. I could see the back of his head and shoulders directly in front of me.

He turned at the rustle of skirts, and his eyebrows shot up when he saw me. Staying low, I darted toward the front of his chair, moving between his legs, low and safely hidden in the darkness of the box.

Moore whispered, "What are you—?"

"Quiet." I peeked up at him. "I only have twenty minutes." I slid my palms over his knees, higher toward his crotch.

He shifted in his seat like he was trying to get away from me. "Rose," he warned softly under his breath, his eyes darting around at the other boxes. "Don't."

I let my fingers dance on his inner thighs. "You came to see me."

He fixed his gaze on the stage, lips barely moving as he said, "I came to see the show."

"Liar." I could see the bulge in his trousers, the heavy weight of him growing larger with each passing second. "You missed me."

"Don't do this."

"Why? No one can see me. And if you keep your eyes on the stage, no one will suspect a thing." I rested my cheek on his leg. "Wouldn't you like to come in my mouth?"

Grimacing as if in pain, he closed his eyes. "It's indecent."

"That's precisely what makes it fun."

"Why are you doing this?"

"Because I missed you, too." I nuzzled his erection through the wool with my nose. "Please, Mr. Emerson?"

"*Shit*," he hissed. "Hurry, Rose. You are needed on stage in sixteen minutes."

Sixteen. Not fifteen or twenty. This man really did pay attention.

With not a moment to lose, I reached for the waistband of his trousers and unfastened the placket. The outline of his hard cock pressed against the fine linen undergarment he wore. The tiny buttons weren't easy, but I made short work of them and revealed the prize underneath.

"Oh, there you are, you gorgeous thing," I whispered as I took out his erection. He was warm and thick in my grip, veins running along the side of the shaft.

I must've studied him too long because he warned under his breath, "Rose."

I placed tiny kisses along the shaft, inhaling the smell of the sandalwood soap off his skin. No doubt the soap was expensive, because men like Moore didn't skimp on luxuries.

I knew men liked when a woman used her tongue, so I made sure to lick Moore all over. I bathed his shaft in my saliva, loving the salty taste of his skin, before I finally slipped the crown into my mouth and sucked on the tip. I felt a shudder go through his big body. Poor man. He needed this so badly.

Determined to finish him quickly, I moved my head up and down, stimulating him with my tongue and lips. I maintained firm pressure, but didn't take him deep enough to make me gag. I couldn't risk my eyes watering and ruining my stage makeup.

I could hear him panting, quiet bursts of air that sounded like they were pulled from his lungs. His thigh muscles clenched beneath my hands, but he didn't move. He let me work at my own pace from the floor at his feet, surrounded by theater-goers. It was one of the riskiest and most thrilling acts I'd ever experienced, but I was loving it. I could hear my fellow actors on stage, reciting their lines, unaware of the very naughty act I was performing up here. My heart slammed against my ribs, the excitement of it a high I hadn't imagined.

I pulled off for a brief second and looked up at him. The skin of his face was taut, his skin flush with pleasure. Such a handsome man. "Can they tell?" I gave him a long lick. "Do they know you're having your cock sucked by one of the actresses?"

He slammed his eyelids shut and grimaced. I fingered the heavy ridge of his crown, enjoying how his member twitched under my touch. "Come in my mouth. I want you to watch me onstage, knowing a part of you is inside me."

"Christ." The one word sounded strangled as he grabbed the base of his shaft and aimed the tip at my lips. "Now, kitten."

I opened wide and took him as deep as I dared. Then I began sucking hard, unwilling to stop until he exploded and gave me his spend. After a minute I felt him tense and his breathing stopped, then ropes of salty fluid splashed onto my tongue and into my mouth. I kept going, determined to take it all, and he kept coming silently, the subtle shudders wracking his frame the only sign of his release.

I held his spend in my mouth when I pulled off. I looked up at him, needing him to see. I waited until he regained a bit of his equilibrium and focused on my face once again.

Finally, he clutched my hand and stared at me with a mix of awe and affection. I said nothing. His brows knitted and he gently brushed the fingers of his free hand along my jaw. "Are you well?" he whispered.

Never breaking our locked stares, I swallowed. Then I licked my lips. "So very well."

"Were you . . .?" He appeared gobsmacked, but this was quickly replaced by arrogant male satisfaction. He rubbed his thumb over my lips. "Did you enjoy my taste?"

"Very much." I needed to hurry back to the stage, but not before I said one more thing. Pulling him forward, I put my lips near his ear. "Thank you for the treat."

## Six

Moore

**THE DAMAGE WAS DONE.** Our path was set.

It was foolhardy to think she wouldn't see me at the matinee. She was too clever, too observant, and now we'd arrived at a turning point.

Two things were abundantly clear. First, I couldn't resist her, and second, we were dangerously compatible. So, why fight it? We were as explosive as gunpowder and both eager adults. The idea of having her in all the various ways I craved gave me a dark, wicked thrill. The city believed me immoral and a scoundrel. Perhaps their opinion had been right all along.

It didn't matter. The two of us would embark on a short, secret affair, just as soon as we did away with her "no repeat" nonsense. A week together, maybe two, should be enough to work her out of my system. And no one would ever know.

Decision made, I skipped the second half of the performance and wandered out into the streets in search of the nearest jewelry store. These things were handled in a certain way and I wished to do it properly. Rose deserved nothing less.

In the store I selected the necklace with the biggest stone, an emerald that matched the color of Rose's eyes. It wasn't as lavish as I'd hoped, so I made a mental note to pay a call to Mr. Tiffany tomorrow.

Once I returned to the theater, the play had nearly finished. The attendants knew me by now, so they didn't protest when I requested to be shown backstage. After being directed down a series of corridors, I found the steps leading to the dressing rooms.

I entered the room with her name on the door, then settled into an armchair in the corner. Resting my derby on my knee, I waited, more content than I could remember. I hadn't felt this light, this *hopeful,* in years. Not since before the divorce proceedings, that was for certain.

Soon I heard a smattering of applause, signaling the end of the performance. There were rumors the show wasn't going to last much longer, and by the dwindling attendance, I believed it. Perhaps she'd take a break from acting and we could sail somewhere on my yacht together. Cuba or Maine, perhaps. Away from prying eyes, alone together.

Finally, after what seemed like an interminable wait, the door opened. Rose entered, her gaze sweeping the room as if she expected me to be here. When she found me, the edge of her mouth curled. "There you are. I grew worried when you left."

"Close the door and come here."

She bit her bottom lip and her breasts bounced provocatively in her low-cut costume as she approached. I moved my derby to make room for her on my lap. "Sit."

Gracefully, she arranged herself on my thighs, shifting the heavy skirts of her costume out of the way. I wrapped one arm around her back and pulled her closer, loving the feeling of her body nestled into mine. With my free hand I produced the jewelry box.

"What's this?"

"A gift that comes with no expectations." I held it out. "But I think it's time we have a serious conversation."

"Oh, I like serious Moore," she teased. "May I open the gift first?"

"Please."

She took the box from my hand and pulled off the ribbon. Then she carefully opened the case to reveal the emerald necklace inside. "Oh, goodness. Moore, this is . . . it's too much. I don't know what to say."

"Do you like it?"

Her verdant green gaze stared at me in awe. "I love it. It's absolutely stunning. But it's too extravagant. You shouldn't—"

I pressed a finger to her lips. "I want you to have it. All you need to say is thank you."

"Thank you," she said softly. "Will you put it on me?"

"Of course." I took the box from her and faced her forward on my lap. Quickly, I slipped the necklace around her throat and fastened the clasp in the back. "There."

She stood and went to the looking glass by her dressing table, where she studied her reflection, turning subtly to the side to let the light catch the stone. "It's gorgeous. It matches my eyes."

"I know. That is why I chose it. Now, come back over here."

Grinning, she practically danced over to where I sat and took her previous spot on my lap. She leaned in and pressed a kiss to my mouth. "I love it. Thank you."

"I'm very glad. You deserve it." I pulled her closer and stroked her leg where it dangled over mine. "Are you ready to talk?"

"What are we discussing? How much I loved it earlier when you—"

"No, not yet. We are discussing us. An arrangement to be specific."

Her eyebrows dipped, a frown marring her flawless features. "Oh. You mean me as your mistress."

"Yes, if you're amenable."

"I told you, I'm not interested in that sort of arrangement. We may have one night of torrid lovemaking, but that's all."

"I want you for more than one night."

"Then you shall be disappointed."

"Tell me your objections to the idea. I promise, I'm very generous."

"It's not about money," she snapped. When she tried to wriggle off my lap, I tightened my arms. "Let me go," she demanded.

"No, not until we have this discussion. Tell me your reasons, kitten."

"Do you believe using an endearment will soften me up?"

"Jewelry and endearments . . . isn't this what every woman wants?"

She rolled her eyes. "You shouldn't generalize. And this woman wants only one thing."

I fingered the lace edging of her bodice and imagined all the delights hidden underneath the cloth. "Marriage and babies then, I suppose."

"Moore. Ugh." She pushed off me and stood, her slight frame rigid with disappointment. "Your opinion of women is deplorable. Is this what those fancy schools teach young boys?"

"No. Mostly they teach antiquated languages and how to dodge a punch. Tell me what you want, Rose."

"Independence."

"But . . . you have it." I gestured to her dressing room. "A career, a life of your own choosing. No husband or father making your decisions."

"I have a career, yes. Except it's fleeting and unpredictable. I'll eventually be too old, and then what will I do? I want something of my own, something lasting. Something that cannot be taken away from me arbitrarily."

She spoke passionately, as if from experience. What had she lost in her past? "Do you want money? Land? What is it you want? Tell me and I'll make it happen."

Instead of answering, she pressed her lips together and shook her head. "I need to do this myself. Don't you understand? That is the very point."

"No, I don't understand. There's no shame in relying on others to help achieve your dreams. The trading of favors is what this city is founded on, for god's sake."

"Is that what we'd be doing? Trading favors?"

"If you wish to consider it like that, then yes. You favor me with your delectable body, and I'll see that you have whatever you wish."

For a second, I thought I had her. The way her eyes went unfocused, as if she were picturing it, made me confident that I'd convinced her. But then she shook her head. "I only sleep with men for fun, not profit. Take it or leave it."

"So I may give you gifts and trinkets." I gestured to the necklace. "But nothing substantial. Do I have it right?"

She began unpinning her hair with ruthless, frustrated movements. "No . . . yes . . . I don't know! This is a lot for me to take in." She threw a hairpin in the direction of her dressing table. "I don't want to be a mistress. Men use sex to control women, to take away our choices. They make promises and then change their minds, leaving us to pick up the pieces."

Oh, I was beginning to understand. This was about her past, not about me. I would unpack that dusty trunk at a later time. Right now I needed to deal with the present.

"Rose, come here."

A sound emerged from her throat, a low furious growl. "See? We haven't even screwed and you're ordering me around!"

I was out of my seat in a blink, pulling her to me and kissing her naughty mouth. I put one hand in her thick curls, the other on her waist, holding her tight, letting her feel my strength as I moved my lips over hers again and again. She softened slowly, her body gradually sagging into mine, until I was practically holding her upright. When her hips pressed closer, I angled my head to deepen the kiss, my tongue finding hers. The taste of her, combined with her sweet sighs, sank into my flesh and turned me as hard as stone.

We finally eased apart, both of us sucking in much-needed air. She was flush and boneless in my arms, her fingers twirling in the overly long hair at the nape of my neck. I could barely restrain myself from undressing her and taking her right there.

I needed her to agree to multiple nights.

"Sweetheart," I whispered against her temple. "I am dying for you. Positively stark raving mad. I'll agree to any conditions you set, provided it's more than one night and we are discreet. You want a bank draft? I'll write it. You want a house? I'll buy it. Tell me what you want from me. I'll gladly give it, free and clear."

She eased back to see my face. "You're serious."

"Of course. I won't ever lie to you."

Her fingertip pressed into the divot on my chin. "Men always lie, especially when their cocks are involved."

God, that word on her lips. Proper women wouldn't dare say such a thing, so hearing it fall from Rose's mouth seemed daring and tantalizing. "Say yes. I'm begging you."

"I do like it when you beg, but I'm sticking to only one night,

Moore. I understand if you want to walk away, though I rather hope you won't."

Failure tasted like ashes in my mouth. Stubborn, stubborn woman. But I hadn't gotten to where I was in this world without knowing how to skirt a rule or two.

I stroked a fingertip along her jaw, feeling the velvety warm skin. "Just to be clear . . . one night of fucking, then I'll leave you be."

"Yes, that is what I'm saying."

"Then I agree."

Surprise stole over her features. "You do?"

I nodded. "Will you sit with me for a moment so that we might discuss when and where?" Instead of waiting, I bent and lifted her in my arms and carried her to the armchair. She wrapped her arms around my neck and held on until I had us settled.

"I've never been carried like that before," she said breathlessly. "I think I like it."

"You think?"

"No, I do. I definitely do."

I made a mental note of this, then arranged her more comfortably atop my thighs. "Now, let's have a reasonable discussion. Do you have a way to prevent contraception?"

"Yes."

"Good. Where do you live?"

"Downtown, on Sullivan Street."

"No, that won't do. I need you closer. Somewhere private."

She rested her head on my shoulder and her fingers fiddled with the studs on my shirt. "A hotel?"

Her tits were driving me mad, the soft flesh pushed high, nearly escaping her décolletage. I plucked at the strings of her bodice, loosening the constricting costume to uncover the mounds underneath. "A hotel is too public, too great a risk. And I want you to be comfortable."

She began helping me, lowering the sleeves as I loosened the fabric. Her breasts emerged tantalizingly slow to my ravenous gaze, until finally one popped free of her corset. Full, creamy flesh tipped with a hard rose-colored point. Christ, she was delectable.

I cupped the mound in my hand and squeezed. "You're so damn

beautiful." Her eyes fluttered closed, the soft lashes kissing her cheeks as I plucked at her nipple. "How do you feel about a townhouse?"

"That seems extravagant for one night."

Moving my lips to her ear, I lowered my voice seductively. "Let me worry about extravagance."

"You want to keep our night together a secret," she said through heavy breaths.

"I don't wish to ruin your reputation or risk your career." As well, the secrecy meant I could shield my mother from any gossip.

I bent her back over my arm and lifted her breast toward my mouth. Leaning down, I licked her nipple a few times, then drew her nipple into my mouth, sucking deep and using my tongue. "I will make you so happy, kitten," I swore against her flesh. "Please say yes."

I bit her nipple gently and she gasped, followed by a long moan. "Oh, god." Her fingers hung onto the back of my head, holding me in place. "Moore, I cannot think straight when you do that."

I released her nipple to murmur, "I want to shower you with pleasure. I want to lick you until you can't stand. I want to give you jewelry and take trips with you. Bend you over the rail of my yacht and—"

A knock sounded on Rose's door. "Rosie, you decent?" a male voice called.

I lifted my head. *Tell him to go away,* I mouthed.

"Not quite, Mr. Martin. If you don't mind, I'll find you in a moment."

"Very well," the man said. "I'll be in my office. Five minutes."

I drew on Rose's nipple again with deep pulls of pressure, and she arched back with a curse. When I slipped my hand beneath her skirts, she parted her legs to let me quickly find her center. Wet and scorching hot, she felt like heaven. I dragged two fingers up her seam to her clitoris. I rubbed lightly, a maddening, teasing brush that would give her a hint of what I was capable of but no satisfaction. Her compliance was what I wanted and I'd go to any lengths to get it.

She rocked her hips, chasing my touch, but I pulled back. "Say yes to the town house," I urged.

"This is hardly fair. You're clouding my mind."

"As you clouded mine today." I used my teeth on her nipple, then blew on it as my fingers increased the pressure between her legs, but only for a second or two before receding.

"Damn it, man," she panted. "I'm so close and you're deliberately drawing this out."

"Say yes and I'll take care of you. In all things, Rose. I'll give you everything your heart desires."

"I don't need—oh, god. Yes! Moore, yes. I agree! Just please . . ."

The words trailed as I pressed hard on the bundle of nerves, giving it friction, and Rose began to orgasm, her limbs trembling. She shouted her pleasure to the empty room, and I was too happy to care whether anyone was listening. Rose was mine. *Finally*.

And all I had to do was keep from fucking her.

# Seven

Rose

LOOKING at the card in my hand, I checked the address. Yes, this was the location Moore had provided.

I shaded my eyes against the afternoon sun and took in the three-story townhouse, with its limestone facade and window boxes full of colorful flowers. This uptown block was quiet, a far cry from rowdiness downtown.

As a love nest went, it was very nice. Was this where Moore brought all of his paramours? It was elegant and sensible, exactly like Moore.

And blasted far. It took me two and a quarter hours by way of two streetcars and one elevated train to get here. Good thing I only needed to make this trip once.

Birds chirped in a tree planted out front, a musical sound, and I found myself smiling. Someday I would own a home like this, a peaceful little slice of heaven with flowers and fences, servants to keep it all nice and neat. A husband waiting for me inside, and he would love me beyond all sense and reason. We would laugh over my outrageous past in the city and he would never judge me or think less of me for it.

*Why would I want to marry a whore who opens her legs to anyone?*

Almost four years later and those words still hurt. Tommy Callan had been the mayor's son and the most handsome boy in Youngstown. He chased me relentlessly the summer I turned sixteen, his actions so attentive and sweet. Except he'd merely wanted under my skirts to claim my virginity, *not* to put a wedding ring on my finger. And I'd been too naive and foolish to realize it.

When I cornered him days later, Tommy set me straight, in public view of the whole town, and I nearly died from the embarrassment of it. My parents couldn't hold their heads up afterward, the shame of what I'd done was too great to bear. They finally told me to leave Ohio and never come back.

The incident taught me a valuable lesson. I could only rely on myself in this world, no one else.

I swallowed all those old memories and walked across the street. As I started up the steps, the massive front door swung open. I expected to find Moore, but instead a man stood there in a fine suit, his demeanor stiff but polite. "Mrs. O'Donahue. Would you care to come inside, please?"

He knew my name.

Feeling foolish, I started forward. "Thank you, yes." I stepped inside the entryway and stuck out my hand. "Hello. I'm Rose."

The man gave me a bow instead of taking my hand. "Mrs. O'Donahue. A pleasure. I am Stewart, the butler."

A butler. Of course Moore had a butler for his love nest. But why was he calling me Mrs. O'Donahue?

"It's miss," I corrected. "And it's nice to meet you."

"It is probably best if we refer to you as Mrs." Stewart gently took my parasol and handbag then placed them on the entry table. "For appearances."

Oh. I hadn't considered that.

"Of course," I said as my cheeks heated. "Mrs. O'Donahue. How could I have forgotten?"

"Excellent. Mr. Emerson is waiting to see you in the sitting room. This way, madam." Stewart walked to a closed door on the right. He slid open the pocket door for me. "Sir, Mrs. O'Donahue is here. Would you like for the kitchen to send up refreshments for your visit?"

"No, that isn't necessary," a familiar deep voice from within said. "That will be all, Stewart."

I went into the sitting room in time to see Moore rise up off the sofa. An explosion of butterflies took flight behind my ribcage at the sight of him. It had been three days since that afternoon in my dressing room, so I allowed myself to drink him in. Dressed finely in a blue pinstripe suit, he appeared perfectly attired, not a rumple or stray hair to be found. Elegance dripped off every inch of his lithe frame, and if one didn't know better, he could pass for royalty. A stately duke or posh earl. I especially loved the hint of gray at his temple, a marking that spoke of experience and maturity.

This was a confident man who knew himself and his place in the world. He never pretended to be anything he wasn't. I could respect it, even if being an actress meant I did the exact opposite.

"There you are." He came toward me as the door slid closed to give us privacy. Placing one finger under my chin, he tilted my face up and placed a kiss on my lips. "I was beginning to think you'd changed your mind."

"How long have you been waiting on me?"

"The better part of an hour." He took my hand and led me to the sofa. "Come, let's sit."

He helped me settle onto a cushion, then lowered himself next to me, never letting go of my hand. "You look beautiful."

"And you look very handsome. Shall we go upstairs?"

"So eager to get in my bed." A small grin played about the edges of his mouth as he rested his arm on the back of the sofa. "I like it."

"That is the reason we're both here."

"Actually, we're here to talk first. There's something I'd like to discuss with you."

Blunt fingertips toyed with the fine hairs at the back of my neck and goosebumps broke out on my skin. "I don't have any diseases and I brought my womb veil."

Dark eyebrows raised ever so slightly. "Practical matters first, I see. All right, then. I'm disease-free as well, and we'll get to the womb veil later. This wasn't what I wished to discuss, however."

"Then what is it?"

"I'm afraid I cannot stay today and defile you as I'd hoped. I must return to the office, then I am engaged for a business dinner."

My face slackened as my mouth dropped open. "You brought me all the way uptown only to send me back downtown? Do you have any idea how long it took me to get here?"

He winced, appearing contrite. "I really do apologize, but I could return after dinner. However, it will be quite late."

"So I'm supposed to sit around in your love nest, alone, waiting until you return."

"Haven't you a show this evening?"

I realized Moore didn't know. "The production closed. That was what Mr. Martin wished to tell me the other day. We're all out of work. But I'll find something else soon." And I would. There were always new shows popping up.

"Then relax here. There's a stocked library. The staff will make you supper. You could take a bath." His fingers skimmed the edge of my jaw in a caress. "And this is not my love nest. I've purchased this town house just for you."

"You bought a townhouse for one night with me?" I rolled my eyes dramatically. "You have more money than sense, Moore."

"No, you misunderstand. I bought this place *for you*. It's yours."

Instantly, I felt dizzy and hot. Had the man not paid a lick of attention to anything I'd said? "We discussed this. I won't be your mistress, living in a house you provide. I won't be dependent on you. After today, we won't see one another again."

Reaching into his pocket, he withdrew a folded paper and held it out. "Read this."

The big black Old English word was as plain as day at the top of the document. "A deed," I mumbled, my brain struggling to take in the document. "It's in my name."

"Yes."

I exhaled, refolded the packet, and held it out to him. "I cannot accept this. It's much too extravagant."

He held up his hands, refusing to take the deed. "I want you to have it, and your living here makes our arrangement tidier. I realize it's an inconvenience for you to uproot yourself and move in, which is why I am willing to pay handsomely for it."

I placed the deed on the tea table and struggled for calm. Struggled and failed. "There is no *arrangement,* you daft man. We are fucking once—*today*—and that's all. I'm not accepting the gift of an Upper East Side townhouse!"

He appeared nonplussed by my tirade, his lips twitching as he stretched out his long legs. "Christ, you're gorgeous when you're mad."

"Ugh!"

Aggravated, I threw up my hands and started to push off the sofa. Moore grabbed my arm to stop me, then tugged me even closer. He captured my face in his palms. "Allow me to give you this. It's a good house on a good street. You won't need to worry over your safety."

"I haven't been worried over my safety in a long time."

"Then allow me to rephrase: *I* don't wish to worry over your safety. I'll sleep better knowing you are here."

"But we hardly know each other. I'm practically a stranger to you."

Sliding closer, he bent to drop small kisses along the side of my throat, then worked his way up my jaw. I relished the scratch of his whiskers, the hot gusts of his breath. Prickles danced on my inner thighs, arousal building between my legs, my anger dwindling. Such was the dangerous power of this man over me.

He rested his forehead on my temple, his mouth near my ear. "You are not a stranger. I watched you night after night for weeks and obsessed over every little detail. You are precious to me, darling girl."

The words sank deep inside me, past the flesh and bone, all the way to my very soul. Had I ever been precious to anyone before? Not even Tommy Callan had said such nice things to me.

Without thinking, I wrapped my fingers around Moore's necktie and lunged toward his mouth, meeting his lips with mine. He gave a small grunt in surprise, then kissed me back eagerly, our lips molding and sliding as our breath mingled. I loved kissing him. Moore kissed like he had all the time in the world, never hurried or rushed. It was far different than my other partners, young men who viewed kissing as a perfunctory step to getting attention on their cocks.

But Moore kissed me like I was his air, his sole focus in life. When his tongue slipped in my mouth, I welcomed it, greeting him with flicks and swirls of my own. He tasted like peppermint, and the cool bite was a sharp contrast to the heat flooding my veins. My pulse pounded in every part of my body, but mostly between my legs. I longed to crawl into his lap and kiss him for the rest of the afternoon.

Suddenly, he broke off. We were both panting heavily, clinging to one another, as the seconds ticked by. "My god, Rose," he rasped. "You have no idea what you do to me. For god's sake, say you'll stay tonight."

The agreement hovered on my tongue. I wanted him desperately—and if I stayed I could talk him out of gifting me with such a ridiculous present. "The staff won't think it strange if I hang about?"

"Darling, I hired the staff to look after you. They will do whatever you like. But don't worry, they are discreet and will disappear when required."

"Whenever you return, you mean."

His smile grew soft and he angled to press a quick kiss on my lips, almost like he couldn't help himself. "Would you rather they hear us fucking?"

The crass word sent another wave of heat between my legs. Just as I was about to agree, I remembered practical matters. "I don't have my things or a change of clothing."

"A few items from Lord & Taylor have been delivered upstairs. If you don't like them, send someone over to Ladies' Mile to get what you want and have them bill me."

I felt my annoyance rise. He'd bought me things from Lord & Taylor? "You knew I'd agree."

"Don't be cross with me, kitten. I am only trying to make this easy for you."

Yes, he was making it *too* easy. He had all this planned out, like a witch dropping crumbs of treats to lure me into his gingerbread house. I needed to keep my head on straight in the face of so much generosity. "Fine, I'll stay. But only tonight."

"Excellent." Slapping his palms on his thighs once, he pushed to his feet. "Stand up and give me a proper kiss goodbye."

"Are you ordering me about again, Mr. Emerson?"

"Don't pretend as if it annoys you. I already know you like it."

Dashed man. I hated when he was right.

I rose and shook out my skirts. Then I drew closer and slid my palms over the hard planes of his chest. I couldn't wait to get him naked tonight, to see the muscles underneath his fancy clothes. This was to be our one and only time together, so I planned to make the most of it.

My arms wound around his neck and I let him feel the heft of my breasts against his body as I sealed our mouths together. I kissed him like a wife sending a soldier off to war, with every ounce of skill and passion I possessed. *Let him think on this during his boring business dinner.*

He soon took over, his tongue bold and demanding, his fingers imprinted in my skin. I held on, desperate for air but unwilling to let him go. The kiss wore on until I was a panting, boneless mess. When we broke apart I was unable to feel my legs. "Goodness," I breathed.

"Indeed." He rolled his hips, and the erection he sported made itself known even through the whalebone of my corset. "I can't wait to fuck you."

"I am very much looking forward to it, as well."

A wicked grin emerged as he stepped back. "Then I shall see you around eleven o'clock, Mrs. O'Donahue."

Moore

## THE NIGHT DRAGGED ON INTERMINABLY.

I'd lied to Rose about attending a business dinner. I didn't wish to hurt her feelings with the truth, which was that I'd promised to escort my mother to the opera. Seeing another production, another actress instead of Rose, felt wrong somehow. It shouldn't, but it did.

The opera was tedious and boring. I longed for the rousing music and laughter of Rose's performance, the lightness I experienced when watching her. She was a delightful break from these dreary, heavy pieces that were popular with the oyster set.

My mind wandered as the singing droned on. Just as soon as this opera ended, I would drop my mother at home then go to Rose. Rose's town house was a mere thirteen blocks from where I lived. I could walk it, if I wished. No one would ever know, and I couldn't bloody wait.

"Moore," my mother said as the crowd broke out into applause. "We have guests coming. Pour the champagne, will you?"

This wasn't unusual. We had one of the biggest boxes on the tier, and she loved to invite her friends in to visit during the intermissions.

"Of course." I helped her to her feet, then led her up the steps and into the salon.

As I was pouring the champagne, guests filtered in from the corridor. Head down, I didn't register the newcomers until my mother said, "Ah, Mr. Whitney-Dunn, Mrs. Cushing. Good evening. And you've brought Gladys, too, I see. How lovely!"

*Goddamn it.* My fingers clenched around the thick glass bottle. Slowly, I angled to cast a disapproving glare in my mother's direction, only she wasn't focused on me. Instead, she was greeting the group warmly, as if they were her long-lost relatives.

I took my time pouring the champagne, both to temper my anger and prepare for this encounter. I must've dragged it out too long because my mother finally said, "Moore, please come and greet our guests."

Refusing was unacceptable, so I turned and presented them with glasses full of champagne. "Sir, Mrs. Cushing. Nice to see you again."

"Good evening, Mr. Emerson," said Mrs. Cushing, who was also Whitney-Dunn's sister. The matron was clearly acting as the young girl's chaperone for the evening.

"Emerson," Whitney-Dunn said. "May I present my daughter, Miss Whitney-Dunn?"

"Miss," I said with a polite bow. "How do you do?"

"How do you do, Mr. Emerson?" Her tone was as bland as tepid tea, her smile flat.

Interesting. Was the lack of enthusiasm mutual, then?

There was an awkward moment of silence until my mother said, "Moore, why don't you take Miss Whitney-Dunn to see the view from our seats?"

This would put the two of us on display in front of the entire tier. The gossip would spread before the end of intermission.

I smothered a sigh. "It would be my honor. Miss, would you care to join me in the box?"

She accepted my arm politely. "Of course. Thank you."

We walked through the salon and into the box. There wasn't much to see, so we both came to a stop near the rail. I glanced at her, surprised by how young she looked in the gas lighting. Was she eighteen? Twenty? With the dewy debutante skin, I couldn't be certain.

But it was clear that she was too young for me.

*Rose is only nineteen.*

I winced. I was too old for both of these young women. Yet I was willing to make excuses for Rose. *Because I wanted her too badly to care.*

"This is a bold, yet obvious ploy, I'm afraid."

Surprised by Miss Whitney-Dunn's comment, I turned to face her. Most young women attempted to play coy with potential suitors. "As a debutante, it can't be the first time you've been subjected to such a ruse, I would imagine."

"Not one quite like this." She studied me. "You have no idea, do you?"

"An idea of what?"

"About my father?" When I didn't say anything, she shook her head. "He is determined for you to marry me."

"It's fortunate, then, that I am of an age when I may make decisions for myself."

"You don't wish to marry me."

Though I couldn't detect a hint of disappointment, I rushed to say, "It is nothing personal. But I have resolved never to remarry, no matter the bride in question."

"I see." She pursed her lips and stared out at the rows of seats. "I must assume your mother is unaware, based on how she discusses you."

"What does she say?"

"That you are ready to settle down and start a family."

I frowned. "She is misguided. A desperate attempt for grandchildren on her part."

Miss Whitney-Dunn gave me a small smile. "You're not worried about my father?"

"Not in the least."

"You'd be the first, then. Every man I meet is terrified of displeasing him."

"I am not every man."

"Yes, I can see." She blew out a breath, her shoulders relaxing.

"Please don't tell my parents, but I'm relieved. No offense, but I am hoping to marry someone closer in age."

"No offense taken. I feel quite ancient standing here next to you."

"Ancient might be an exaggeration, Mr. Emerson, considering that early every woman on the tier is ogling you at the moment."

I suspected it had more to do with watching Gladys and me together rather than my looks. "Shall we return to the salon? I daresay we've fulfilled our obligations."

"Of course." We went into the salon together. The older couple was speaking quietly with my mother, making plans, no doubt. All three glanced up at our return, their expectant glances examining us.

Mrs. Cushing made excuses for her and Miss Whitney-Dunn, leaving me and my mother alone with the elder Whitney-Dunn. When my mother excused herself to visit a friend along the tier, I braced myself. It was clear Whitney-Dunn had wished to get me alone, and I suspected the thread of the conversation.

"You and Gladys seem to get on well," he began after finishing his champagne.

"She's a lovely girl." I went to retrieve the cold champagne bottle from the bucket. "You'll have no trouble finding her a match this spring."

"Moore, I'm not one to prevaricate, so let's be frank. I want you and Gladys married before the end of the year."

I returned and filled both our glasses. Too bad there was nothing stronger than champagne on hand. "If we are to be frank, sir, then I will tell you a marriage won't happen. I have no intention of marrying again."

"Yes, I'm told that is the case. The scandal and all that nonsense." He waved his free hand, as if the worst period of my life was nothing but a trivial exaggeration. "However, I plan to change your mind. You need a son to ensure that Emerson Holdings continues to thrive after you're gone. Your father understood this, which is precisely why he spent most of his life preparing you to take over."

The reminder of my father was a sharp pain under my ribs. "There are many qualified employees who are capable of—"

"That's downright blasphemy and you know it." His bushy white sideburns quivered in his outrage. "You oversee the fortunes of many important families in this city, mine included. Do you think we will allow just anyone to get their hands on them? People want an Emerson in charge, Moore. Someone of our class, someone who understands the implications."

"People, meaning you."

"People, meaning the Emerson Holdings Board of Directors."

My muscles tightened and I strangled the glass in my hand. So Whitney-Dunn was planning to turn the board against me if I didn't do what he wished. "Harold," I said seriously. "I don't appreciate being threatened."

He shook his head as if I were a foolish child. "And you don't seem to understand the gravity of the situation. Your father died eight years ago, Moore. He was fifty-one years old. You're almost forty. The board is growing concerned."

"It's far too soon for panic. I will ensure the business is in good hands before I die."

"No one knows how long they have on this earth. You could die tomorrow and where would that leave us?"

*Not grieving for me, obviously.* Rather everyone would be worried about their money, which is all this city seemed to care about.

Perhaps I was reading this wrong. Was Whitney-Dunn trying to gain a foothold into the company by making me his son-in-law?

I decided to test my theory. "What if I already have someone in mind, someone I'd like to marry who isn't your daughter?"

His eyes narrowed into tiny slits. "Who is she? I've heard of no one attached to your name."

Still playing along, I said, "It wouldn't be right for me to disclose the lady's name without speaking to her first. In any case, it doesn't matter. If your only concern is my legacy, then you may rest assured I have it in hand."

He stared at me for a long moment, his face inscrutable. But I could tell he was trying to assess whether I was telling the truth or not. Finally, he said, "My daughter will make you an excellent wife. Your father would have approved of this match."

Now I knew this wasn't about my legacy, but rather *his.* "Except my father's not here, is he?"

Whitney-Dunn's neck turned scarlet, his lips thinning. Just as he opened his mouth, however, my mother reentered the salon. "Oh, Harold. You're still here."

"I was just leaving." After one last angry glare at me, he turned and kissed my mother's cheek. "We'll speak later, Charlotte. Good evening."

After Whitney-Dunn departed my mother picked up her champagne glass. "Well?" she asked when the silence stretched.

I didn't pretend to misunderstand. "I don't appreciate an ambush."

She waved her hand, the diamonds on her fingers and wrist glinting in the soft electric lighting. "Nonsense. You'd never have agreed otherwise."

"That's correct. We discussed this. I don't need your intervention in my personal life."

"There's no need for you to be cross, Moore. I'm only trying to help you. A mother doesn't like to see her son all alone in the world with no one looking after him."

But I wasn't alone. I had Rose. And the sooner this blasted night ended, the sooner I could feast on her delectable body. "I'm perfectly happy, mother. I don't need anyone to look after me."

The lights flickered, and I was eager to put an end to this topic for good. "Let's retake our seats. The second act is about to start."

# Nine

Rose

## THE HOUSE WAS QUIET.

I wasn't used to so much silence, even at night. It unnerved me and I twitched at every little noise as the hours progressed. My world consisted of voices behind walls and sounds through open windows, music from nearby saloons. Carriages and carts rumbling up the street. Hooves clattering on cobblestones.

This was an eerie stillness, one reserved for the wealthy.

The staff had been accommodating, just as Moore predicted. I expected judgment and scornful stares, considering the reason for my being here, but I'd received none. Merely friendly nods and deferential treatment. It was a relief, a welcome contrast to how I'd been treated back in Youngstown.

Then there were the "few items" Moore had ordered from Lord & Taylor. For a man who dealt with numbers all day, he had a serious problem with counting. An entire wardrobe was waiting for me, with dresses for every occasion as well as undergarments. There were even hair pins, nightwear, shoes and bonnets. I couldn't believe my eyes. Was he planning for me to move in?

The idea of it nearly gave me hives.

As the clock approached eleven, I fidgeted and paced. I drank a glass of wine. I undressed and bathed, then brushed out my hair. I'd even inserted the womb veil.

There was nothing else to do but wait.

Should I get in bed? Remove my clothing? Wait for him downstairs? Pour him a drink? This wasn't my home and I wasn't his mistress. The whole thing was unnerving.

I took several deep breaths. This was ridiculous. *It's one night. Calm down.*

I decided to be comfortable, so I found a book of Shakespeare's plays and crawled into bed. At least this way I wouldn't be watching the clock.

Not much later I heard footsteps on the stairs. Before I could set the book down, the bedroom door opened and Moore emerged. My breath caught. *Dear lord*, he looked handsome. He wore a formal black evening suit, with a white silk vest, and tie, his long limbs and strong shoulders on display in the fine wool. His hair was perfectly arranged, his jaw firm with determination. This was the Knickerbocker scion, the powerful man who had everything at his fingertips.

I couldn't wait to see the real man underneath.

The edge of his mouth kicked up—Moore's version of a wide smile —and he closed the door behind him. "I like you waiting in bed for me."

Trying to calm my racing heart, I set my book on the nightstand. "Lucky for you that I'm still awake."

"Were you bored?" He removed his jacket and tossed it over a chair back. "I apologize for being late."

I couldn't let the opportunity to undress him go to waste, so I threw back the covers and stood. His fingers stilled on his bowtie as his eyes locked onto my breasts, which were barely covered in a thin linen night-dress. I put a sway into my hips as I approached him, knowing it made my flesh bounce enticingly.

"Your hair," he whispered as I stopped in front of him. "It's so unique, so lovely." He curled a long lock around one of his fingers.

I went to work on the buttons of his vest, the planes of his chest rising and falling beneath my fingers. "Thank you. You're very handsome, Mr. Emerson."

"Are you wearing drawers?"

I glanced up at him, delighted at the feverish light dancing in his eyes. A rush of longing and lust went through me, wetness pooling between my thighs. I bit my lip. "No."

"Christ." He grabbed the linen of my nightdress and yanked it up. "I need this off. *Now.*"

I lifted my arms and the fabric disappeared in a sweep of linen. Then I was naked in front of him, with nothing to hide me from his intense gaze. I shivered.

One large hand covered my breast, while the other stroked my hip. "You're stunning, kitten. Absolutely stunning."

Humming, I leaned into his touch. "Compliments are my very favorite thing."

"Is that so?" He rolled my nipple between his fingertips—and I sucked in a sharp breath. "And I thought my mouth between your legs was your favorite thing."

"Second favorite thing, then."

His lips curled, his expression positively devious. "Get on the bed."

I didn't delay.

I crawled onto the coverlet and flipped onto my back. I didn't hide. Instead, I propped up on my elbows and unabashedly observed his disrobing, while Moore kept his eyes on my breasts, the skin of his throat flushed as his chest bellowed with his breaths. Quickly, he removed his vest and bowtie, then his shirt collar and cuff links. All the trappings that made him a gentleman. An erection tented the front of his trousers and I was very much looking forward to getting my hands— and mouth—on his thick length once again.

"Keep going," I told him. "Now it's your turn to put on a performance for me."

"Impudent girl." He whipped off his shirt, but kept his union suit on. "Christ, I can't stand it a moment longer."

He was on me in a blink, covering my body and pushing me into the mattress. His mouth took mine as he wedged his hips between my thighs. He kissed me as he always did—full of greed and hunger and *devotion*. I felt cared for and protected with this man, not like a temporary lover.

I sank into the kiss, relaxing and letting him stroke his tongue over mine. Moore was a good kisser and he knew how to build the desire between us. My thoughts scattered and I focused only on his mouth and the delicious heavy weight of him atop me. My hands clutched his shoulders, my hips rocking, seeking of their own volition. There was so much I needed in that moment and Moore was the only man who could give it to me.

He broke off and bent to take the tip of my breast into his mouth, drawing the taut nipple onto his tongue. Liquid fire raced to my groin, the pressure from his mouth echoing between my legs. "Oh god, Moore!"

He hummed against my skin and shifted slightly. Then I felt his fingers gently sliding through my folds, probing until he reached my center. I was slick and sensitive, desperate for him to fill this emptiness inside me. But he didn't rush. He stretched me, mouth sucking on my breast, until I was rocking on his hand, begging. "Moore, please. I cannot take this teasing. I need you."

He switched to my other breast and added another finger. This was a tighter fit, but there was no pain. Only fullness that didn't quite reach where I wanted. Then he began using his thumb on my clitoris, circling, and I clutched his head as the pleasure mounted. "Moore," I whined, drawing his name out.

Ignoring me, he kept at it. Soon I was trembling, panting, the sensations too much. "Yes, yes, oh god!" The orgasm rushed under my skin, little shocks that started in my toes and spread to every part of me. I trembled, lost in the high of his touch, my fingers digging into his muscles to stay tethered. When I finally stopped convulsing, I sagged onto the mattress and Moore was there to kiss me so sweetly.

"I'll never tire of watching you find your pleasure. You are gorgeous, sweetheart."

I could barely catch my breath. "Moore, please. Undress and let me feel you inside me."

His eyes closed as if he were in pain, his erection digging into my thigh. "Later. I'd like something else right now. Get on your knees. Take me in your mouth."

Excitement bubbled in my chest, prompting my limbs into action. I scrambled to my knees and started working on his undergarment. When I had the union suit unbuttoned I freed his erection from his clothing. I licked my lips at the sight of his cock. Indeed, this was a superlative specimen. Smooth and long, with enough girth to stretch my mouth wide. How were the ladies of Fifth Avenue not chasing him about everywhere he went?

I wrapped my hand around the base of his shaft and looked up at him. His gaze glittered like flames, the lines of his face pulled taut. He'd lost his smooth veneer; this was a man on a knife's edge, uncivilized and raw. It was heady, knowing I had done this to him, and I wanted to see him completely undone.

He placed his hand atop mine and angled his crown toward my lips. "Open."

At his rough command, I lowered my jaw and slid out my tongue. Moore dragged the head of his cock over my tongue, around and around, wetting the skin with my saliva. "God, you are exquisite," he whispered, sounding almost angry about the fact. "The most beautiful creature I've ever seen. I hadn't a hope of holding out against you."

He pressed onto my tongue, robbing me of the chance to respond, as his shaft tunneled into my mouth. I accepted the width of him, stretching, making sure to keep my lips over my teeth. He tasted like skin and man, and a hint of salty fluid coated my tongue. A pleased moan rumbled in my throat.

"Perfect," he murmured. "You are so damn perfect. Let me all the way in, my sweet Rose."

I took as much of him as I could, then he thrust up, giving me even more. "Fuck, that's nice," I barely heard him say over the sound of my own breathing. He stroked the top of my head. "Lick me, little kitten. Prove to me how much you want it."

This required no acting skills on my part. I did want him—desperately. Moore was rough and filthy, and he sparked a previously undiscovered part inside me, as if he were setting blaze to all the expectations and assumptions I'd ever held. Finding the strength to walk away tonight would *not* be easy.

I shoved all those thoughts aside and began licking him, bathing his length with my tongue. I gave him long swipes, as well as tiny flicks —anything to show my reverence, my devotion this one last time together. I worshiped him without shame. I captured the beads of fluid leaking from the tip, and I dug into the sensitive ridges on the underside. I dipped my head and nuzzled the heavy twin weights below. I used my breath and my lips on his balls to make his thighs tremble.

Slight pressure on my head forced me to stop, so I looked up at him. "It's time," he panted, eyes wild. "Suck me deep and fast. Hurry."

I slid him into my mouth and used the tightest suction I could manage, while my nails dug into his hips. He thrust up as I worked, his crown hitting the back of my throat every time. Then he held my head with both hands and began working up a rhythm. My eyes watered, but I kept my jaw wide, as wide as I could possibly manage, with my tongue scraping the bottom of his shaft.

A few additional deep strokes and he was panting. "I'm going to come," he choked out. "I can't—*fuck!*"

He began climaxing in my mouth, thick spurts that coated my tongue. His big body shook and twitched, but I clung to him, unwilling to let go until it was over. I swallowed and swallowed, drinking him down, my throat working to take everything he gave me, while I continued to watch him.

When he finished, I pulled off and tried to catch my breath, my head resting on his thigh. His eyes remained closed, but he petted my hair, stroking me affectionately. I was burning up, pulse pounding between my legs, my body demanding satisfaction once again.

Which was why I found it disappointing when he tucked himself inside his clothing and buttoned his union suit. "Come here."

I crawled up his body and settled next to him, my head resting on his arm. "Are you dressing to leave already?"

"No. I thought I'd stay here with you tonight."

Oh. I hadn't spent the night with a lover before.

"Are you disappointed?" he asked.

I tried to sound confident. "Of course not. I am curious, though, if you normally stay over with a woman you've bedded."

He turned toward me and slid a heavy thigh between my legs. One large hand settled on my hip. "I haven't bedded you."

"Semantics. You know what I mean."

"I haven't, no."

"Did you sleep in the same bed as your wife?" Most high society men didn't, from what I'd gleaned.

"She preferred to sleep alone."

"That sounds lonely. Did you love her?"

He was quiet for a moment, his chest rising slowly with his measured breath. "It was never about love. The match was a duty, nothing more. And we got on, never argued. There was a routine, a predictability about it that I appreciated. She wasn't passionate, but I tried to ensure she enjoyed our infrequent couplings. I thought . . ." He cleared his throat. "I thought I was doing everything right. I was honestly surprised when she demanded the divorce. I never planned for the marriage to end."

My heart twisted at the idea of Moore living such a colorless, boring existence with a woman who didn't appreciate him. He deserved laughter and love, someone to make him smile instead of frown. Someone to bring him picnics at work and shake up his life.

He stroked my spine with his palm, up and down, up and down, almost as if soothing me. I could feel myself growing tired. "You could have refused the divorce," I pointed out.

"My parents had a happy marriage. I foolishly believed I'd have the same. Keeping Eugenia trapped in a marriage she didn't want felt . . . cruel." He paused for a beat. "She said I was the coldest person she'd ever met."

*Oh, my poor Moore.* I angled to press a kiss to his jaw. "You don't seem cold to me, darling."

He bent his head and gave me a long lingering kiss on the mouth. "The newspapers were even worse. They called me every name in the book when the chorus girl took the stand and revealed all my supposedly sordid secrets."

"That's awful. Especially when you were doing this to grant Eugenia her freedom. What did they say about you?"

"They called me an adulterer and immoral. There were stories about orgies I attended. It was utterly humiliating. And why I'll never marry again."

I could only imagine how much a proud man like Moore had suffered through the public mudslinging. Though he had a gruff exterior, Moore was soft and sensitive underneath. "They're just words, Moore," I said quietly as I stroked a thumb across his cheek soothingly. "And you know they aren't true."

He kissed me again. "You sound as if you're speaking from experience."

"A bit, yes. Back in Youngstown, there was a boy. The mayor's son." Moore grew very still, but I stared at his chest as I spoke. "He was full of praise and sweet words. Chased me all around town one summer. He even gave me a promise ring. He claimed we would soon make it official and there was no reason not to anticipate the wedding night."

"*Son of a bitch.*"

Moore's curse produced a grim smile out of me. "Indeed, I haven't many nice things to say about him either, not after refused to marry me. Apparently, when a woman doesn't bleed her first time, she's not a virgin. He made sure to let everyone know."

"Oh, Rose. I'm so damn sorry."

I attempted to shrug, like I wasn't still hurt. "I expected the holy rollers to shun me, of course, but I never thought my parents would throw me out."

"They did? That's terrible."

"It was all too much for them. They needed to pretend I didn't exist."

"Don't defend them," he said quietly. "At the very least they should've supported you."

"You of all people are aware of how ugly public disgrace becomes." I toyed absently with the hair on his chest. "Not every parent is able to handle the weight of it."

He went still and I wondered what I'd said wrong. Was it about his parents? I leaned back to see his face. "Moore—"

"The scandal with Eugenia. It killed my father."

My lips parted on a swift intake of breath. This couldn't be true. It was too horrible to contemplate. "What do you mean?"

"Halfway through the trial, when the newspapers sank their teeth into me, he dropped dead one evening. No warning, his heart just gave out."

"But that might've happened regardless. You can't know that the trial was the cause."

"You didn't see him in those few months. He was angry and so bitter. Disappointed in me. He tried to talk me out of it a hundred times. Said I was a stain on the family."

"Oh, darling." I moved closer and hugged him. "You did a very noble thing. I'm sorry you suffered for it."

He pressed his face into my hair and we stayed there for a long moment. "Tell me how you came to New York, how you became the great Rose O'Donahue."

"I had no money when I came to the city. Thankfully, I found a cheap room in a ladies' boarding house and one of the girls there sang in the chorus of a Broadway show. She made it sound so glamorous and easy. With her help, I auditioned for an upcoming show and they hired me on the spot."

"That's astounding. But then, you're immensely talented."

"Thank you, but it was about being in the right place at the right time."

"A little bit of luck, then," Moore said.

"Indeed. Someday I hope to find a way to help the girls pouring into the city to start new lives for themselves. So many are preyed upon by unscrupulous characters."

"Would you serve as a theatrical agent or a producer?"

"I'm not sure. Perhaps."

"I've no doubt you'll succeed in whatever you set your mind to." Moore yawned, then stretched his arms over his head. "You're quite remarkable, Rose."

My stomach dipped and swirled as I watched him move. Lord, but he was a sight, all solid bone and muscle, his hair rumpled from my hands. And his wife hadn't wanted him? Was she cracked?

If I had this in my bed every night—

I swallowed that thought. I wouldn't have him except tonight. This wasn't an affair or a courtship, and I wasn't a mistress or a wife. We were two people enjoying a tiny bit of heaven in a split second of time.

That was all.

I waited until he drifted off to sleep before whispering, "I think you're quite remarkable, too."

# Ten

Moore

**I WOKE FIRST.**

Not entirely surprising, as I got out of bed every morning at dawn. An old habit from my father that I inherited. The soft weight next to me, however, did startle me. I hadn't expected to find myself tangled up with Rose like a ball of string, but our limbs intertwined at some point in the night, our bodies holding fast to each other as we slept.

*You don't seem cold to me, darling.*

I stared at the ceiling. This woman—this feisty, dazzling actress— was slowly working her way under my skin, down into the parts I never shared with anyone. I wanted to protect her and ravish her and hear every word that comes out of her blasted mouth.

More than anything, though, I didn't wish to leave her.

I needed to make my way home to ready myself for the office. In the last eight years of running Emerson Holdings I hadn't been late once. In fact, I was often the first one to arrive and the last one to depart at night.

So, why couldn't I move?

I dipped my head and buried my nose in her hair, inhaling deeply. Roses.

"Are you sniffing me?"

Her voice was rough with sleep, but laced with amusement. I smiled into the soft red strands. "Is that a problem?"

She burrowed deeper into my side, her feet rubbing along my calf. "No, as long as you don't move and let me sleep another four or five hours."

"I'm afraid that's not possible. I have work today."

"But don't you own the company?"

"I am the president, but I answer to the Board of Directors." As Whitney-Dunn was so helpful to point out last night.

"Then stay with me." She pressed her lips to my chest, gifting me with gentle kisses. "We can have breakfast together. After, of course."

"After?"

"After you screw me."

My cock, already stiff from her presence, grew even harder at her words. "Is that what you think will happen?"

Rose's hand slid along my stomach, over my union suit, and cupped my erection. "Yes, I rather do."

I rolled her onto her back and leaned over her, pinning her hands to the mattress. "You seem quite confident about this."

She wrapped one leg around me, grinding her bare pussy against my thigh. "I feel very confident."

I captured her mouth kissing her roughly. I wanted to fuck her. Desperately. The need was always under my skin, scratching and clawing, demanding to be satisfied. But I wouldn't. Not yet.

This was a battle of wills between Rose and me, except I was far more stubborn. I was a numbers man, someone who understood probability. If I fucked her right now, the likelihood that I would never see her again was too high. She had to trust me first. So I wasn't fucking her until she agreed to many nights together.

I slid down her body, brushing kisses over her soft skin as I went, until I reached her pussy. I knew how much she loved this, as did I, so I licked her, sucked on her clitoris—even bit her gently—until she was nearly sobbing for a climax.

"Moore, *please*. Put yourself inside me."

Climbing up the bed, I braced my back against the headboard, but didn't take off my union suit. I grabbed her waist, lifted her, and helped her straddle my hips. "Ride me, kitten. Make us both come."

She started to reach for the buttons of my undergarment, but I stopped her hand. "Grind down. Use my cock to climax."

Her creamy skin flushed as she began rocking her hips. "I want you naked."

"There's no time," I lied. "I'm too close." Her tits bounced in my face, so I suckled on her nipple, running my tongue and lips over the velvety tip. Rose didn't waste time. Instead, she used her legs to work up a rhythm, lifting, sliding, and each drag of her center along my shaft caused me to see stars. I held onto her hips and tried to hold off the orgasm building in my lower back. "It feels so good," I groaned against her breast. "*Goddamn*, woman. Hurry."

Sweat turned her skin slick, the morning light streaking across her limbs like she'd been dipped in gold. Rose threw her head back, eyes closed as she sought her peak. She was the most beautiful woman I'd ever encountered and I would fight like hell to keep her in my bed as long as possible.

"Oh, god. Moore. Yes, yes, yes!"

*Thank Christ.*

As Rose started to climax, I let myself go. Pleasure stole through my veins, the force of it causing my vision to go white behind my eyelids. Spend shot out the tip of my cock, soaking the cloth that separated us. It went on and on, my muscles convulsing as the pulses rocked my frame.

She collapsed atop me, appearing not to mind the wet linen between us. Her head nestled into the crook of my neck and I wrapped my arms around her back, holding her.

"That felt amazing," she whispered.

"Yes, it did." I closed my eyes and let my head fall back. My body hummed with bone-deep satisfaction.

"You're avoiding bedding me."

"Why would I do something so foolish?"

"Because you know I won't agree to see you again."

Clever woman.

I decided to be honest with her. "Here is the truth, then. I want to fuck you more than my next breath. But I won't, not until you agree to whatever this is between us."

"Become your mistress, you mean."

"Lover, paramour, bed partner, friends who occasionally screw . . . There are several names by which I may refer to you that are not *mistress*." I held the back of her head and forced her to look at me. "I have money, sweetheart. I want to use it to spoil you, shower you with trinkets and baubles, if only to make you smile. I want you safe, here in this town house, not struggling with streetcars and crowded apartments. I want to feast on your pussy until I can't see straight, then fuck you every which way I know how. The arrangement between us is our decision alone and no one else's concern."

I could see emotion in her green depths, but it was tempered. As if she were smothering the feeling with ruthless intention. "You make it sound so easy," she finally said.

"Because it is. Money makes things easy, sweetheart, and I have loads of it. We'll have our fun and both walk away the better for it."

For a split second I thought I had her convinced. But then the stubborn woman eased out of my grip and off my lap. She rubbed her bare arms, her chin high. "Tonight, Moore. We both return here and finish this."

Sighing, I watched as she grabbed the dressing gown from the wardrobe and disappeared into the washroom. I wasn't so easily defeated.

Rose and I weren't finished, not by a long shot.

# Eleven

Rose

**THE EARLY FEBRUARY** winds threatened to take my hat several times as I hurried through Union Square. I regretted not taking a hansom, but I was trying to save my money. The walk helped to clear my head.

It had been a week of late nights with Moore at the town house. Seven nights of sweaty grinding and kissing that never quite satisfied the place inside me that longed for him. True to his word, he hadn't bedded me—no matter how much I begged. He never entered me, never joined our bodies together. The frustration was driving me out of my skull.

And worst of all? I was developing feelings for him.

These were deep, lasting feelings, the type I'd avoided since Ohio. I was the world's biggest fool. Why was I so self-destructive in my choice of men? Tommy, the mayor's son, never intended to marry a girl like me, one from a poor family. And now Moore, an unattainable man from the highest social echelon. The world in which the Emersons lived consisted of strict social rules for associating with the "right" types of people. In both cases I was the good time, the woman they lusted for, but would never keep.

Staying with Moore, allowing our arrangement to continue, meant only heartache. Yet I couldn't keep away. I returned each night to the town house to meet him, where I let him undress me and have his wicked way with me. I was utterly weak when it came to him, powerless to resist the pull between us.

It would be easier to let go if this was purely physical. But we talked late into the night, either in bed or the bath. There was something so calm and steady about Moore. In some ways he was my opposite, but we were alike in many others, too. Like our ambition, our need for financial security. Our love of ice cream and distaste for meringue. I made him laugh and he gave me investment advice.

And the heat between us was an inferno.

"Hey, stranger!"

The nearby voice brought me out of my tangled thoughts. Glancing around, I broke out into a huge smile when I spotted a familiar face. "Flora!" We embraced quickly. "It's good to see you."

"Same, Rosie. I'm still disappointed that our show closed last week. We had a lot of fun together."

"Yes, we did. Are you auditioning already?"

"I am. You know how it is. No rest for the wicked."

I grinned. "Indeed, such is the life we lead. I'm off to an audition, as well. Are you headed over to Sixth Avenue?"

She nodded once and took my elbow, then we started walking. "It's a small part for *In Gay New York*. One of the actresses has throat problems, so they need a replacement quick." She bumped my shoulder with hers. "You know, it's in your vocal range and you're about her size. You should come for an audition."

"I'll think about it. Right now, I'm off to see Mr. Martin. He's looking at leads for *The Bathing Girl*." This upcoming production was well-financed and rumored to be the "it" show of the autumn. Fortunately for me, my former director was at the helm.

"Lucky you!" Flora exclaimed. "This could be your big break as a lead actress."

"I know. Cross your fingers for me."

"I'll cross my fingers *and* my toes!" We walked in companionable silence until she asked, "What happened with your uptown swell?"

"Mr. Emerson. We're . . . friends."

"Friends, as in the kind who stay overnight together?"

Was I going to admit this? It felt strange, even if Flora was a good friend. "Yes. That kind."

Flora whistled. "Holy crackers. You landed a whale. Good for you! Is he doing right by you?"

The comment took me by surprise. I hadn't been trying to land Moore. I was trying to have one night of passion with him and move on.

Except I wasn't quite trying. My will to resist him melted like warm butter every time he touched me.

"He's merely a friend," I explained quietly. "As I've said, I don't wish to become a rich man's mistress."

"I know, but I don't see anything wrong with it. If the situation were reversed, would it matter?"

"I don't understand."

"Meaning if you had the money. Because if I were wealthy, I would gladly support a man to dote on me night and day."

"I don't mind the doting, per se. But if I come to depend on him, what happens when he decides we're over? Men are unreliable and selfish."

"Oh, so Emerson is one of the cheap ones."

We turned a corner and a fierce wind blew around the ornate buildings. I burrowed a bit deeper into my coat and, for some inexplicable reason, rushed to defend Moore. "No, definitely not. He bought me a townhouse near the park."

"Sakes alive! A townhouse! And near the park?" She huffed a cloud of white in the cold air. "You've barely met and already you're acquiring real estate. Now I'm truly jealous."

"I can't accept it." I cast a quick glance at her. "It wouldn't be right."

She shook her head as if confused. "I don't understand. Is the town house temporary or conditional in some way?"

"No, he put the deed in my name. But it doesn't feel right to take Moore's money and gifts, when I don't deserve them."

"Rosie." Flora stopped in the middle of the walk and grabbed my arm. Her expression was full of disbelief under the rim of her bonnet.

"Do you think there is a man alive who has refused a favor when it's been offered? That is how the entire city works!" She swept her arm out to the buildings. "If a man went to Yale or went to Harvard. If he frequents the same club you frequent. Or comes from the neighborhood in which you grew up. It's all in who you know and what you can trade that matters."

*Money makes things easy, sweetheart, and I have loads of it.*

Moore's words echoed in my head and I wrinkled my nose. "I know you're right," I told Flora, "but I promised myself that I'd remain independent. When I came to New York, I swore to rely on only my skills."

"Except you are relying on your skills—the kind of skills a man appreciates."

I couldn't help but laugh. "You know what I mean. My *acting* skills."

She grew serious, her eyes kind. "Honey, we're taught we can have control over our lives, but it's an illusion. Tiny coincidences and chances occur every day to affect our opportunities and decisions. As Shakespeare says, 'Fortune brings in some boats that are not steered.' Sometimes good things happen, even when we don't believe we deserve them, and we still must grab onto those chances with both hands."

"You would quote my favorite of Shakespeare's obscure plays."

"You can't argue with the Bard." Flora took my arm and we started walking again. "Think about it. You're off to see Mr. Martin. You're hoping to leverage the familiarity you have with him to land a role in his new show. That is favoritism, Rosie."

"Yes, but I worked hard in our last production. And I'm a damn good actress."

"Of course you are. But that's the most coveted role on Broadway. I heard even Sarah Bernhardt was sailing in from Paris to audition."

"*She is?*" Good lord, I hadn't expected such fierce competition.

"It's what I heard. However, you have a leg up because you are friendly with Mr. Martin."

Hmm. I hadn't ever considered it like this. Still, I wasn't sure I agreed when it came to Moore. "So you think I should become Mr. Emerson's mistress. Throw all my good sense to the wind and use him for whatever trinkets and townhouses he bestows on me?"

"You're not using him. You're bringing some much-needed joy and passion to that sour man's life."

"He's not sour!"

"You forget I saw him in that box for almost a month. I don't think he smiled even once!"

True, Moore didn't smile much. But I'd coaxed multiple smiles out of him the past few days. I treasured each one, because he seemed so lonely deep down, a man dedicated to his company and nothing else. Maybe he did need me.

Flora nudged my ribs. "I know that expression. I've seen a similar look on just about every actress's face at some point. You are fond of him."

"Well, of course I'm fond of him. I wouldn't agree to his arrangement if I weren't."

"No, I mean very, very fond. Deep-down-to-your-toes fond."

We reached my address, so I drew to a halt. "You're wrong. We're merely friends. Furthermore, I'd be a dashed fool to develop feelings for him."

"I don't know," Flora said thoughtfully, her lips pursing. "Maybe you two will have a grand love affair. It'll be like *The Shop Girl*, except instead of marrying the poor medical student, you end up with the millionaire."

The possibility was ludicrous. As much as I wished otherwise, men from Moore's world married women of their own class—not that Moore would ever remarry. He was firmly against taking another bride, which shouldn't have mattered to me.

But it did.

Shoving aside thoughts of marriage, I said, "I'd rather make my own millions."

Flora rolled her eyes. "Who wouldn't? But you know how you make millions? Real estate. Take the town house from Mr. Emerson and sell it if you want. Use the money to start a business or better yet, buy another house. Or buy an apartment building where struggling actresses can live cheaply and avoid the lecherous landlords."

We both gave a tiny shiver at those words. Nearly every actress I knew had been cheated or propositioned or threatened by a male land-lord in this city. "You're full of sound advice today, Flora. Thank you."

"I hope you listen. And if you buy that apartment building, please send a word. Because I will move in before the ink dries on the deed!"

"I will," I said with a chuckle as we embraced. "I'm so glad I ran into you today. Good luck in your audition."

"You too, Rosie. I have a feeling that great things are about to happen for both of us. And don't forget the Bard!" She waved then hurried up the walk, disappearing into the throngs of people.

*Fortune brings in some boats that are not steered.*

I thought about this line, my eyes going a bit unfocused. Had Moore been brought into my life for a reason? Was I a fool for standing on my principles when he was freely willing to give me a townhouse? And Flora was right about trading favors. Whether it was stock tips, job opportunities, or construction bids, this city worked on graft and kick-backs, whispers and favors.

Was it wrong for a woman to want to get ahead, too?

Acting paid well, but I couldn't afford a townhouse on the park. As Flora said, I could sell it later and set myself up for a lifetime of financial security. Also, I hadn't been to my tiny apartment downtown in four days. Moore had provided me with an entire wardrobe, everything I needed to live in the town house. The servants deferred to me, and it was beginning to feel more comfortable, like my own home.

Who was I fooling? I was already a mistress. Not allowing Moore inside my body meant nothing when he was inside my heart and mind. In fact, it was growing increasingly difficult to be apart. I longed for him whenever we weren't together, physically ached for his presence.

I inhaled and filled my lungs with bracing cold air. Letting it out slowly, I stared up at the limestone office building, determination settling into my bones. I was an actress first. Even as Moore's mistress, I wouldn't give up my career. Because he wouldn't stick around forever. I had to keep that in mind as I charted these new waters.

I started for the entrance, ready to call in my favor.

# Twelve

Moore

I RESISTED the urge to glance at my pocket watch. The tedium of this dinner was nearly unbearable. There was only one place I wished to be—and it wasn't in the main dining room at Sherry's.

Rose's town house had become my second home. I spent every night with her, then rose early to return home and dress for work. This week has been the best of my life. Rose and I were perfectly suited, our interests and preferences aligned. She was smart, funny, and bold. I felt lighter in her presence, then rejuvenated afterward, like she was a dry cell battery for my spirit. I don't know how I'd endured the last thirty-eight years without her.

"Did you hear me, Emerson?"

Clearing my throat, I forced my attention off thoughts of Rose and back to Whitney-Dunn, who'd requested this dinner. He expected me to admit to not listening, but I could pay attention and long for Rose at the same time. I'd been doing it for a month, after all.

"For god's sake, do not buy silver," I said immediately. "We're still attempting to recover from the devaluation last year."

Whitney-Dunn wiped his mustache delicately with the serviette. "May I speak plainly?"

"Of course. I like to think we've always done so with one another."

"Indeed, we have." He folded his hands and stared at me directly. "I relayed your feelings to the board several nights ago. They are displeased."

"Oh? I wasn't aware of any board meeting."

He waved his hand, as if this was unimportant. "It wasn't official, but most of us happened to linger at the Union Club."

Happened to linger? I didn't buy it for a second. "And what was discussed without the board president in attendance?"

"Now, there's no need to be prickly with me, Moore. I've known you since you were born, your father long before that. Everyone has your best interests at heart."

Wrong. This was about the best interests of the company. "This is about your daughter."

"I want to hear your objections to the match."

Doubtful. More like he wished to argue with me and browbeat me into doing as he wished. Indeed, I was not easily browbeat these days. "I am not a child, Harold. I won't be badgered into another marriage."

"Moore," he said, heaving a sigh. "The business with Eugenia was a long time ago. The trial may have been unpleasant for a few months, but you have an obligation to your shareholders and clients."

Unpleasant? Try humiliating to my very bones. And it hadn't been months—it had been *years*.

But to be clear, this wasn't about any obligation. Whitney-Dunn wished to gain a foothold in Emerson Holdings through his daughter. As my wife's father, Harold would have a greater influence, possibly even force me out.

I wouldn't have it.

Leaning in, I met his steely gaze with one of my own. "My obligation is to myself first and foremost. The shareholders and clients are in good hands. I've never failed them, nor do I intend to do so in the future."

The silence stretched and Whitney-Dunn's frown deepened. Relaxing, I sipped my drink and waited for him to continue or drop the subject.

Finally, he said, "Moore, there is talk."

The muscles behind my shoulder blades tightened. Memories of whispers and stares still haunted me. "Regarding?"

"An actress. Living in a town house you paid for."

I shouldn't have been surprised, yet I was. How had this become known? While I hadn't tried to hide the presence of a woman in my life —a man sleeping out night after night tended to mean only one thing— the details behind my arrangement with Rose were private.

There was only one answer. "Are you having me investigated?"

Whitney-Dunn crooked one eyebrow at me. "A very young actress, I might add."

I ground my back teeth together, furious. "I don't care for what you are implying, Harold. Miss O'Donahue is of legal age. Furthermore, nearly every man we know has a mistress. Why is this worth remarking upon?"

"Because it's unusual for you. It speaks to a concerning level of commitment, one that doesn't reflect well on you or the business."

I took a healthy swig of whiskey, letting the burn slide all the way to my stomach, steadying me. "This is coming from the board, I suppose, all of whom are faithful to their wives."

"Now, there's no reason for such maliciousness. The board is concerned that with mistresses and actresses come . . ." He waved his hand. "Extravagance."

I let out a huff of outraged disbelief and rubbed my eyes. Now they were calling into question my integrity? "No doubt you are stoking their worst fears."

"Why would I do such a thing when the obvious solution is right before our very eyes?"

*Marrying his daughter.*

Fucking hell.

"A solution that benefits you above anyone else."

He held up his hands, placating me. "I cannot pretend to hate the idea of having my grandchildren inherit Emerson Holdings. And no one is telling you to break things off with this actress. My daughter will make you an excellent wife, Moore. Gladys will look the other way to your private life."

*Immoral.*

*Adulterer.*

*Scoundrel.*

The words from the trial haunted me. I couldn't escape them, no matter how hard I tried. Was this what everyone expected of me?

"I would honor my vows," I snapped, "should I ever be stupid enough to repeat them again. But the whole notion is absurd. Gladys has as little interest in marriage as I do."

"Gladys will do as she's told. We must maintain our class and standing. The undesirables flood our streets by the thousands every day, and we must protect our way of life or see it disappear. Your mother understands this, as does the board. It's your responsibility to ensure the future generation, to secure the legacy of the company."

"Do not lecture me about responsibility," I gritted out from behind clenched teeth. "I have given everything I have to the business since the day my father died."

"That was around the time of the scandal, was it not?" Whitney-Dunn angled in his chair, crossing his legs. He toyed with his crystal tumbler on the white tablecloth. "His heart seemed fine before the trial. A strange coincidence, wouldn't you say?"

My mouth dried out. The pain in my chest grew sharp and precise, like an arrow to my sternum. "I should punch you for making such an outrageous suggestion."

"But you've wondered about it, haven't you? I can see it on your face. Any son with half a heart would consider the possibility."

Of course I had. Whether or not the trial was responsible, the stress of that circus couldn't have done my father's heart any favors.

But Whitney-Dunn wasn't finished.

"A man of your age," he insisted, "should be settled, growing a family. Instead, you're spending nearly every night with a nineteen-year-old actress. Wouldn't you like to ease your mother's worries? She is getting older, her health not what it once was. Think of what another Emerson scandal might do to her." He paused. "Or worse. Think about what losing the company would do to her."

Now it was clear he was having me followed, goddamn it.

"The only one concerned about my whereabouts is you," I forced out, pleased with how even my voice sounded despite my growing rage. "And I don't appreciate your threats."

"These are not threats, I assure you. This marriage will happen, because I'll stop at nothing, absolutely nothing, to see it through. No matter how many theater owners I need to pay off and board members I need to bribe."

Theater owners? I knew he was exerting influence—through either intimidation or bribes—over the board, but the comment about paying off theater owners made no sense. "Why would you involve yourself with theater owners?"

"Because I want you to know what I'm willing to do. Your ladybird will have a hard time finding another production willing to hire her, if you don't agree to marry Gladys."

The abrupt closing of Rose's last show. Christ, I couldn't believe it. "You had no right to interfere in such an underhanded and malicious way."

"I'm trying to help you!" He smacked his palm on the table, rattling the china and glassware, as well as attracting attention from our neighbors. "Your mother isn't well, and you're gallivanting around the city with a girl young enough to be your daughter. Wise up, Emerson!"

Everything around me slowed to a crawl, my vision tunneling to Whitney-Dunn's face. "What did you say?"

He grimaced and avoided my eyes. "Which part?"

"About my mother's health. What isn't she telling me, Harold?"

Tapping his fingers on the tablecloth, Whitney-Dunn sighed. "I promised her I wouldn't say anything. She doesn't want you to know."

"Except you did tell me, so now I need to hear all of it." Scenarios bounced around in my brain, each one worse than the last. I didn't want to lose her, either. "Is it her heart? Her breathing? Cancer?"

"It's her heart," Whitney-Dunn confirmed. "She's getting light-headed and there is some irregularity in the rhythm of her heartbeat."

My chest caved in, my lungs unable to draw in air. Was Whitney-Dunn lying to me? It had seemed a genuine slip of the tongue, but one could never know.

Then I remembered our exchange the night she waited up for me.

*What happens after I'm no longer here?*

*That's twice you've mentioned your death. What aren't you telling me?*

Swallowing my panic, I vowed to follow up with my mother's physician at my earliest opportunity. As soon as I left this restaurant. I knew where Dr. Fritz lived. He was also my physician.

"It's to be expected at her age," Whitney-Dunn said. "But the doctors have advised her to rest and not overtax herself. That includes outside stressors, I would imagine. Perhaps like a son embroiled in a second public scandal."

"Then I'll sever my relationship with Miss O'Donahue." Or at the very least, I'd carry on discreetly. "Which would solve the problem."

"Certainly you can, but it won't affect a marriage to my daughter. I don't care if you carry on with that actress tart or not. You will marry Gladys before the year is out, Moore. Or I'll strip that company away from you, even if it puts your mother in an early grave."

Shocked, I stared at this man. "You were my father's close friend. How can you hurt his wife, his family like this?"

"I am trying to make you see reason, for Christ's sake. Gladys will be a good wife. The two of you will produce heirs to take over Emerson Holdings, and you may live your life outside of that however you see fit. Your actress can continue to work, and your mother will continue on until her dotage, untouched by scandal. How is this hurting anyone?"

The patrons in the dining room blurred before my eyes to a pale watercolor of conformity and obligation. I felt backed into a corner, a narrow confined space of Whitney-Dunn's making. I didn't want to agree, but I couldn't see a way out. A refusal to marry, though reasonable, would harm the two most important women in my life. How could I sacrifice both my mother and Rose on the altar of my stubbornness? Whitney-Dunn held all the power between us, and I couldn't risk my mother's health through a scandal or losing the company.

And Rose . . . She'd never forgive me if I were the reason she couldn't find work in this city. She would move away to Boston or Philadelphia. Worse, maybe she'd go as far as Chicago. Though we hadn't officially slept together, it was only a matter of time before I convinced her. I couldn't lose her, not now. Perhaps not ever.

Still, the agreement for the marriage wouldn't come. The words were stuck in my throat.

When I couldn't stall any longer, I finished the rest of my drink and set the tumbler on the table. "We'll reconvene after I speak with my mother's physician. If what you've said is true, I'll call on Gladys." Tossing my serviette onto the table, I pushed my chair back and stood. "However, if I find out you've lied to me, there isn't a hole small enough in which to hide, Harold. I'll bury you."

"Noted." Whitney-Dunn already appeared pleased with himself, hands folded over his stomach, a broad smile on his face. "I'm proud of you for doing the right thing, Moore."

I didn't bother responding or shaking his hand. I crossed the floor and departed the dining room swiftly. I needed to be far, far away from Whitney-Dunn and this restaurant. Indeed, there was only one place I wished to be at the moment.

And it wasn't at home.

# Thirteen

Rose

I MEANT TO SEDUCE HIM. Instead, I fell asleep.

Some mistress I was turning out to be.

I blinked as the bedroom door opened. Moore strode in and I struggled to a sitting position. The book I'd been reading in bed fell off my chest and dropped onto the floor. As he came into full view, I could see Moore looked haggard, grumpier than usual. "Did you have a rough night?"

"You could say that," he murmured and tossed his overcoat onto a settee. Then he began ruthlessly attacking the buttons of his top coat.

Clad in only my silk nightgown, I slid out of bed and hurried toward him. "Here, let me. You're going to rip a perfectly fine garment." I shoved his hands out of the way and began to undress him.

His fingers traced patterns over my bare arms. "I apologize for coming here so late. I had errands to run after my supper concluded."

"Oh?" Maybe this explained his mood. "I hope everything is alright."

His chest rose and fell under my fingertips as I unbuttoned his vest.

"Christ, you're beautiful," he whispered, his knuckles skimming my jaw. "I never get tired of looking at you."

"You are quite handsome yourself, Mr. Emerson." I held up his wrist and removed his gold cufflink. Then I repeated this on his other wrist and dropped the gold pieces onto the carpet.

He settled a hand on my hip. "You were worried about my coat, but toss the cufflinks like they're hairpins?"

"You can replace the cufflinks. But we both know you aren't mending that topcoat yourself."

"I'll be sure to tell my valet. He'll be pleased to know he has such a champion in you."

"He must suspect you have a lady friend, considering you haven't been sleeping at home." I set about removing his collar and studs.

Moore lifted his chin to allow my fingers room to work. "Darling, there is very little he doesn't know about my life."

"Does he know about me, then?"

"I believe I may have shared it. Does that bother you?"

I bit my lip, strangely pleased at the idea of Moore confessing his interest in me to his valet. "No. I spoke to my friend Flora about you today."

"Is that so?"

I nodded. "It was a very illuminating conversation."

His finger paused on its slow journey into my décolletage. "Meaning?"

A giddy excitement bubbled up inside me, a happiness I always felt in Moore's presence. Except tonight would change everything between us . . . and I couldn't wait. "I'm yours, Moore."

"Do you mean—?" He sucked in a sharp breath. "I need to hear you say it."

I met his gaze steadily. "I've decided to be your mistress."

"Oh, thank god," he said a beat before lowering his head to seal our mouths together. He kissed me hard, urgently, but with a singular focus and finesse. There was nothing like this man's kisses. I could drown in them and die happy.

Suddenly, he broke off and lifted me in one smooth motion. In seconds I was flat on my back, atop the bed, with him covering me.

Leaning on one elbow, he swept the hair off my face, his eyes soft as he stared down at me. "You are aware that I adore you, that I can barely think straight when we're apart? I promise that I am going to make you so goddamn happy, sweetheart."

My stomach gave a little flip as my chest expanded with tenderness. "You had better."

"Are you ready for me to fuck you tonight?"

"More than ready, as soon as I put my womb veil in."

He rested his forehead on mine and closed his eyes. "Go. Hurry. And take off that dashed nightgown. I need you naked as quickly as possible."

I kissed his cheek, then edged away from him. "I'll return in a moment. You best be naked, too."

The last image I had of him before I shut the washroom door was of Moore shoving off his suspenders and wrestling with his shirt. Inside the washroom I hurried with the cream and contraceptive device, then I removed my nightgown and placed it on the hook fixed to the back of the door. Completely bare, I walked into the bedroom.

Moore paused in the process of shoving his trousers off his hips. "Fuck. You are an absolute goddess. Come here." He kicked off the fine wool and stripped off his socks, leaving him in his thin undergarment. As usual.

I gestured to his frame. "Completely off. I'm not playing this game any longer."

Coming up on his knees, he smirked as his fingers flew down his chest. Buttons popped and the edges of the undergarment soon parted to reveal his strong chest coated lightly in dark hair. I'd seen him naked, of course, but not until after we were finished, either while sleeping or in the bath. I couldn't wait to see him in a fully aroused state.

"Keep going," I encouraged. "I want to see every bit of you."

He stopped, then let his hands drop to his sides. "You want my cock? Crawl over here and get it."

I didn't hesitate, starting for him. I didn't mind taking orders from Moore in bed, a fact he was aware of.

Once on the mattress, I crawled on my hands and knees toward him. His eyes focused on my breasts, which were heavy and sensitive, as I moved slowly across the coverlet. When I reached him I kissed his bare stomach. Then I licked his thick erection through the thin cotton, teasing him. His hand slid through my hair and cupped the back of my head. "Show me how much you need it, darling."

I was an actress, so I could perform when needed. But this required no acting on my part. I really did need him. I was delirious for him, panting and dizzy, with my pussy wet and throbbing. Nuzzling his shaft only made it worse, because I knew this would be inside me soon. "I need it, baby." I nipped his cloth-covered crown with my teeth. "Fuck me, Moore. Fuck me and make me yours."

"Shit," he hissed as a shudder ran through his big body.

Suddenly, I was on my back, his lower half settling between my thighs. "I can't wait another second." He reached between us. A few more buttons popped and his undergarment was open. Then he had his shaft in his hand, angling the head toward my entrance. "Stop me if it hurts."

He nudged my opening, spreading my arousal over the crown, before easing inside, widening me. Stretching me. Filling me up with his glorious thickness. I threw my head back, enjoying every centimeter he gave me.

"Look at you," he whispered. "Sucking me inside for the first time. That's it, kitten. Let me in and I'll make you feel so good."

There was no pain, just wonderful pressure. "Keep going. I need all of you."

He groaned, a tortured sound. "God, you're so tight." He gave a small thrust, burying himself deeper, as his thumb began making circles on my clitoris. "So damn tight."

The little swipes of his thumb distracted me from the heavy length of him invading my body. It was quite a lot at once, and it quickly turned from nice to incredible. I angled my hips, rolling, eager for him, and then finally he was there, taking up all the space inside me. Goodness, it was better than any other experience in the past.

He angled over me to rest his palms on the mattress, then stared down at me, his concerned eyes studying my face. "Good?"

"Please, you need to move. I'm burning alive."

He began thrusting, slow at first, his hips barely moving. But the pace quickly increased, his length sliding across my sensitive tissues, then bottoming out again. Moore built up a rhythm, his big body moving, straining, and I joined him by rocking my hips to meet his. We were no longer two separate people; we were one, our muscles and limbs working toward the same goal.

My insides coiled, everything pulling tighter and tighter as the pleasure built. I clutched anywhere I could reach and dug my nails into his skin, desperate to hold on. Our grunts and exhales mingled into a single lewd symphony, and watching him use his body to pleasure us both sent me higher. He was fierce and relentless. His hips slapped against mine with each stroke, which caused the bed to rock and creak. I didn't care who heard us. I wouldn't have wanted him to stop for anything in the world.

This was nothing like the impersonal couplings of my past. This was intimate, with Moore deep inside my body as he surrounded me. It was the two of us, together. Nothing else mattered in this moment, such as labels or money or whatever the future might bring. Right now, I was his and he was mine.

The orgasm slammed into me, the wave dragging me under and tossing me about. My walls squeezed around his cock, my limbs convulsing, and my vision sparkled behind my eyelids. "Oh, god," I whispered before letting out a long moan.

Moore's hips stuttered and he shouted, "God, Rose!" Then he thrust deep, like he was trying to burrow inside me, and I felt him swell and grow thicker. He threw his head back and his whole body shuddered. I didn't dare miss a second of it—I loved watching Moore fall apart. He lost his society trappings, the rigidity and pompousness of being a wealthy tycoon. In this moment he was merely a man, *my* man.

Finally, he sagged, his chest heaving, as tiny aftershocks rocked his frame. "Damn it. I hope I didn't hurt you."

"I'm fine. Fit as a fiddle and ready to go again."

He chuckled, then withdrew and dropped onto the bed beside me. "I may need a few moments."

I rolled to kiss his jaw. "Then I will clean up and allow you to recover." I needed to deal with the womb veil. The midwife said not to leave it in for too long after a man spent inside me.

"Hurry," he said, eyes still closed and one arm thrown over his head. "I want to hold you."

My heart melted a little and I patted his stomach. "I'll be right back."

Once in the washroom it took me longer than anticipated to deal with the womb veil and clean myself. I knew it would get easier over time, though. When I returned to the bedroom I found Moore fast asleep.

I stood by the bed and tried to memorize every detail. He was so handsome, even while sleeping. The sharp lines of his face were relaxed now, the dark hair mussed from my hands. Lips slightly parted with his deep breaths. His union suit was open and pushed down his hips, his skin dewy with sweat. My heart melted, happiness threading through my chest like vines. I liked seeing him so relaxed, so comfortable. It was a far cry from the man who'd tried to kick me out of his office all those days ago.

Very carefully, I dragged his union suit off his legs, leaving him naked. Strong muscles roped his long frame, while dark hair dusted his arms and legs, as well as his chest. There were no flaws, no marks. He was perfect from head to toe, the ideal male specimen. Unsurprising with Moore being an Emerson and all. God forbid, they were anything less than the best.

Smiling, I crawled into bed next to him and drew the covers up. I moved closer to feel him and let his body warm me. The instant I was beside him he rolled toward me and threw an arm around my waist. "Look your fill, kitten?"

Ah, so he'd been awake. "No, not nearly. Will you walk across the room for me? Maybe turn slowly once or twice?"

He gave a weak huff of laughter. "Tomorrow, I promise. For now, sleep beside me and let me hold you." He kissed the back of my head. "Thank you for tonight. And thank you for being mine."

*Being mine.*

I liked that. Far too much.

No one had ever wanted me enough to keep me. The entire town, including my own family, had turned their backs on me during the scandal. So I came to New York alone and worked hard to become a successful actress. It hadn't been easy, but I made a name for myself—a new name that I'd chosen. Rose Doyle no longer existed.

I didn't know what the future held for Rose O'Donahue . . . but Mr. Alfred Moore Emerson III was a part of it.

"You're welcome," I whispered back to him. "And thank you for everything, baby."

"You don't ever need to thank me. I'm the luckiest man in this godforsaken city."

I snuggled closer to him. "You're very sweet after climaxing."

His chest shook with laughter. "Only with you." He rubbed my hip for a long moment, then said, "Come sailing with me on my yacht tomorrow. I want to have you all to myself for a few days."

This was surprising. "Can you miss work?"

"I can bring the work with me."

"Then yes, I'll come sailing with you." It sounded like heaven, and there was no reason to stay in the city at the moment. I wouldn't hear back about my audition for a few weeks, Mr. Martin had said.

"Excellent. We'll leave after my morning meeting."

"Oh. Did you need to wrap up at the office?"

"Something like that. Now, get some sleep. Because I will definitely need to fuck you again before I go."

Grinning, I let myself drift off, already anticipating tomorrow.

# Fourteen

Moore

I SAT IN THE DARK, staring out at the black ocean surrounding the boat. A glass of whiskey rested on my knee. An awful feeling had settled in the pit of my stomach, one I couldn't shake.

I was an engaged man.

Earlier today, I paid a visit to the Whitney-Dunn residence. With both my mother and Gladys's father watching carefully, I asked Gladys for her hand. The girl had agreed and I gave her the ring I purchased from Mr. Tiffany last night. Whitney-Dunn had hired a photographer, so Gladys and I then posed for a portrait to appear in the newspaper this week.

I wanted to howl with the unfairness of it. Punch something, rip apart the city with my bare hands.

*There hadn't been a choice.*

The truth was little consolation to having my choices stripped away.

Unfortunately, my mother's physician confirmed Whitney-Dunn's information. Her heart was failing. It could be a week, it could be a month. Even years. No one knew how much longer she had, but I wouldn't add to her worries by having the company stripped away or creating another scandal. I couldn't lose her as I'd lost my father, and marrying Gladys prolonged my mother's life. It also kept Whitney-Dunn and the board off my back.

And I got to keep Rose.

Some of the bitterness and frustration eased from my muscles. Rose had finally agreed to be mine and I was goddamn grateful for it. It certainly lessened the sting of having this matrimonial decision forced upon me.

Lifting my glass, I drained half of it.

Perhaps it wouldn't be so bad. I'd have a son or a daughter, maybe more. There would be someone to manage the house. And just as soon as Gladys was pregnant, I could devote my time to Rose.

*Adulterer.*

Yes, I would be. And I'd feel absolutely no regret over it, not if it meant keeping Rose. Gossips be damned. They didn't know what she and I shared, what Rose made me feel. I could never survive without her. She was a source of happiness and light, the only joy I had in this miserable world. I couldn't bear to face a day without her.

Now I had her all to myself for almost a week. It was purely selfish on my part, but the thought of staying in the city, accepting congratulations for a marriage I didn't want, had been too much to bear. So I dragged Rose off to my yacht, content to hide away from the rest of New York for as long as I could manage.

As if I'd conjured her from my thoughts, her voice sounded from across the room. "Darling, what are you doing here all by yourself?"

My lips tilted at the corners. "My beautiful Rose." I opened my arms and she slipped onto my lap, fitting perfectly into my body. I kissed her temple. "Why are you awake, sweetheart?"

"I woke up and missed you." She took the glass from my hand and finished my drink. "Whiskey. Mmm, delicious."

I cupped her hip and nestled her closer. "I tried to be quiet when I left."

"I didn't hear a thing. Why are you out here drinking? Is something wrong?"

The words wouldn't come. I knew I needed to tell her, but I wasn't ready. Telling Rose meant it was actually happening.

*It appears in the newspaper in two days. Everyone will soon know.*

Still, I wasn't ready to face it. I was a coward, clearly, but I just needed one more day before I spoke the words to another person. "It's nothing. Merely thinking."

Her fingers trailed along my jaw. "Do you wish to talk about it?"

"Not really."

She slid her nose against my cheek. "Have I told you how much I adore your yacht?"

"Several times, but I'm pleased to hear it. We will be spending a lot of time here."

"Oh, we will? That is quite a bold assumption, Mr. Emerson."

I loved when she called me by my surname. There was something so proper, yet teasing, in the way she said it. Naughty, almost. "Are you complaining?"

"No, though I do hope to be working again soon."

I remembered Whitney-Dunn's promise to keep Rose unemployed. At least this was no longer an issue. "Have you been offered a part?"

"Not yet, but I auditioned for my former director yesterday. He told me I have a very good chance."

"What's the production?"

"*The Bathing Girl.* It opens on Broadway this autumn."

"Bathing? Will you be naked in a brass tub on stage?"

"I don't know. If it's required of the role, then yes."

I frowned, unsure how I felt about that. I didn't want men leering at her night after night, though it was hypocritical of me to say, considering I'd spent a month leering at Rose from the audience.

What bothered me more was the timing. I was to marry in late September. I needed to see Rose if I hoped to survive the wedding obligations.

"You grew quiet," she remarked. "Do you have a problem with the show?"

"No," I said hesitantly.

"Then what are you thinking? But before you answer, I have to say I won't allow you to dictate which roles I accept. You and I have an arrangement, but I still possess a mind of my own. And this is a Broadway lead. It could be a big opportunity for me."

I rubbed her bare legs under her silk nightgown. "I know, but . . . Would you consider taking time off from acting? We could sail to Bar Harbor or Newport this summer." Of course this was unfair of me to ask, but I couldn't help it. My whole world was about to turn upside down and this woman felt like a port in a storm, a refuge.

"I prefer to work, Moore. I cannot laze about all day, waiting in bed for you to arrive. I need to keep busy."

"I promise to keep you very busy."

I slid my hand higher until I reached her inner thigh, but she shoved my hand down to her knee. "Stop. You're in a strange mood tonight. Are you drunk?"

I almost wished. "No."

"Then please explain your high-handed, selfish behavior."

"You're right. I am being selfish and high-handed, but can you blame me? You've only just agreed to be mine. I need to fulfill every fantasy I've had of you since the night I first saw you perform."

"That's sweet of you." She nuzzled my jaw with her nose, sending goose bumps along my skin. "You're very sweet, Mr. Emerson."

I clutched her tighter, and the confession suddenly tumbled from my lips. "Rose, I am lost without you. When you smile at me the world sparkles, bright and shiny, like a black curtain has parted from around my eyes. I haven't felt like this with anyone before, not in thirty-eight years. It's why I returned to see you night after night. And now that we've slept together, the feeling has only intensified. You've turned me inside-out, woman."

"Moore," she breathed, sliding her fingers into my hair. "It's the same for me. I've never felt this close to anyone else, not even my family. I don't understand how it happened so quickly, but you're . . . *everything*."

My chest expanded with emotion. The words made me feel fifty feet tall. A skyscraper, towering above the mere mortals below. My god, what had I ever done to deserve this intelligent, beautiful woman?

Still holding her in my arms, I rose and started for our cabin. "I need to kiss you properly in a bed. Preferably for hours."

"That will make sleeping a challenge," she teased, nipping at my earlobe.

I tossed her over my shoulder, which produced a squeal from under her curtain of red hair. I slapped her buttock once. "An Emerson is always up for a challenge."

*Part Two*

Rose

## "I AM ENGAGED."

Time slowed to a crawl. Unseeing, I blinked several times into the bright sun shimmering off the ocean. I must've misheard. This had to be a mistake. Or, was I still asleep and caught in a terrible nightmare?

I spoke carefully, enunciating every word as if I were on stage. "You are *engaged?*"

Moore grimaced, unhappiness etched in every tiny line surrounding his mouth. He squeezed my hip as if to reassure me. "As I said, it's naught but a nuisance. Nothing for you to worry about, really."

"You are getting married."

"Yes. In September."

"Married," I repeated, numbly.

"The engagement party is a week from Saturday."

His voice was so calm, so cool. Like he was telling me what was on the evening's menu. Yet the words tore me up inside, razor-sharp slashes of pain I hadn't expected. I eased to a sitting position, making sure we were no longer touching. I couldn't think what to say, so I asked, "And who is the lucky woman?"

"Miss Gladys Claypoole Whitney-Dunn."

"Goodness. So many names." Hadn't I made the same remark upon meeting Moore? Short names were far too common for the families in Moore's world. Otherwise, how does one brag about one's lineage?

I shook myself. Why on earth was I focused on names when Moore was *remarrying*?

I couldn't believe it. I didn't *want* to believe it. Why hadn't he told me he was searching for a bride when the topic came up earlier this week?

*I will never lie to you.*

Such was his promise when attempting to bed me, words that meant nothing, obviously. Ever since we met, he made it clear that he'd never remarry. A lie, and now I had slept with another woman's fiancé.

Carefully, I slid out of bed and found my dressing gown on the settee. I was too brittle, too raw to conduct this conversation in the nude. When I was covered I turned and faced him. "We discussed this only the other night and you expressed your resolve to never remarry. What changed your mind?"

"It doesn't matter."

"Indeed, it does."

He drew himself to a sitting position and rested against the headboard. He rubbed his jaw for several seconds, like he was debating his answer. "It was the lesser of many evils," he said cryptically.

I struggled to breathe, my heart thumping in my ears. Clearly, Moore intended to withhold his reasoning. And why would a powerful, rich man like Moore confide in me? He hadn't bothered to inform me of his search, so why tell me the reason behind the change of heart? I was merely the woman he paid for his convenience, the available doxy.

*You are his mistress, not his wife. Not even his friend.*

I was a fool.

My heart, the useless organ, cracked and shattered inside my chest. This was precisely why I'd never wished to become a mistress in the first place. His words last night meant nothing. I wasn't important to him, nor had he developed feelings for me. Only I had been so senseless, so careless as to fall in love.

But one thing was for certain: Moore would never know of my true feelings for him. He would never learn how much he'd hurt me in this moment.

The ability to bury my personal pain had served me well and allowed me to become an actress—a damn good one, too. Rose O'Donahue knew how to put on a performance.

My stomach roiled with misery, but I took a deep breath. I could do this. I could pretend and keep my head on straight. And I would survive losing him. I'd survived far worse in my short life. I would not break, not over this.

No man would break me.

I wiped my expression clean. "And when is the joyous event?"

"The twenty-second of September."

I gave him a wide smile. "My congratulations to you both. She's a lucky woman."

His eyes examined me carefully. "You're certainly taking this well. I feel as though I'm more rattled by the whole business than anyone else."

Indeed, how *awful* for him. Gaining a wife to take care of his needs, as well as his home. Provide him with children and never complain. Yes, a man's lot in life was certainly a pity.

None of this was Moore's fault, however. I was the buffoon for thinking him mine, for allowing my heart to attach itself to him.

"And you needn't worry," he was saying, swinging his legs over the side of the bed and standing. "I plan to move you farther uptown, closer to my new home."

"New home?"

He dragged a hand through his hair. "Probably somewhere around Ninety-Third or Ninety-Fourth Street. I still want you within walking distance."

I swayed as dismay shot through me like an electric charge. Did he honestly believe our arrangement would continue after his marriage?

My acting skills must've failed me, because Moore frowned as he watched me. "You don't care for the idea of living uptown?"

We stared at one another for a long beat, the tension pulled tight between us. Grief and frustration—and anger—gathered in my chest like a storm cloud. I angled away from him and stared at the opulent cabin around me, the gold fixtures and the priceless paintings. The mahogany panels, the stained glass.

*I don't belong here.*

I clutched the lapels of the dressing gown around my naked flesh. Cold seeped under my skin, down to my bones, but I needed to remain strong. "Moore, this won't continue after you've married."

His eyebrows flew up. "You and me, you are saying."

"Yes."

Still naked, he folded his arms across his chest. "Why the hell not?"

*Because I would die inside, a little bit at a time. Day by day, week by week, until there was nothing left.*

Squarely, I met his gaze and let him see the truth of what needed to be said. "I cannot remain your mistress after you marry. It goes against all my principles—and *yours*. Remember the gossip after the trial? The names they called you?"

"No man in my world honors his marriage vows. That isn't how it's done, Rose."

"Are you attempting to convince yourself or me?"

The skin of his throat turned a dull red as his mouth flattened. "It doesn't matter because I won't give you up."

Oh, so this was his decision alone? The absolute *nerve* of him. "I'll not come between a wife and her husband. Miss Whitney-Dunn deserves better."

"You don't even know her."

"That isn't the point!" God willing, I would never meet or see Moore's fiancée. "I won't help you dishonor your vows. You hated what happened last time and you hadn't even strayed. Imagine how awful it will be this time when it's *true*."

"I don't give a good goddamn!" he all but shouted. "You are worth the gossip and whispers. They may call me whatever names they like. I won't give you up, Rose."

A fresh jolt of pain stole my breath. He actually expected me to stay, to share him with another woman. A wife, who carried his name and his children. Lived in his home and attended events with him. *Slept* with him.

Me? I wasn't worth marrying. I was the trollop he fucked—and I would never be anything else, to hell with my feelings.

I couldn't help but feel like Rose Doyle back in Youngstown, hoping for a man to love her enough to marry her. Longing for a partner who would stand before God and the world and claim her. Instead, I'd been used and cast aside, humiliated—and now it was happening all over again.

I was stronger now. And I wouldn't let anyone have power over me. I was Rose O'Donahue, for god's sake. A girl who'd left home with almost nothing and became a successful actress. I would never beg for crumbs of a man's attention. So I would enjoy Moore for the time we had left, then turn him over to the woman with too many names to remember.

Quietly, I said, "I cannot share you with a wife. I won't do it, Moore."

He stared out the window, giving me his handsome profile. I loved looking at him, noting the various expressions he wore, the hint of gray at his temples. But another woman would soon own that pleasure, and I needed to bear it somehow.

A muscle jumped in his jaw. "You are aware I don't love her, correct? This is an obligation, nothing more."

"Which is immaterial to our discussion. Carrying on after your marriage hurts everyone."

He began pacing, his tendons and muscles taut with anger. "This isn't a marriage I want. I'm being forced to marry her. Do you understand? This is not a joyous occasion."

"I doubt Miss Whitney-Dunn shares your perspective on the matter."

"Then you'd be wrong. When we spoke, she was less than thrilled at the prospect of marriage."

This didn't console me. In fact, it only confused me. "Why are you marrying her, then?"

"Because I have no choice!"

Moore, not have a choice? I didn't believe it. There was something he wasn't telling me.

I struggled for calm, determined to get answers. "You told me you would never marry again. Explain, then, how you are being forced to go back on your word."

He put his hands on his hips and stared out the porthole. "It doesn't matter. It's out of my hands."

"Then in whose hands does the decision rest? Because I cannot believe you are agreeing, considering your strong feelings on the subject matter."

"Rose . . ."

He let my name trail off, once again reluctant to confide in me. Gone was the man from last night who had been so forthright and open. This was another shift between us, secrets and decisions that were none of my concern. He had a future to think about, one that didn't include me.

Nausea swirled inside my belly and I knew I needed time alone. My stomach and head were a mess, not to mention my heart. I turned on my heel and started for the door.

"Where are you going?" he asked.

"On deck. I need some air."

"But it is cold out there and you're hardly dressed."

I didn't mind. I was frozen inside, anyway.

"Shall I come with you?" he asked as I pulled open the door.

"I'd prefer if you didn't. I'll be fine."

And I would be. Eventually.

## Sixteen

Moore

ROSE WAS SUBDUED DURING SUPPER, quiet and seemingly lost in thought. I had expected it after our argument, though I still tried valiantly to coax her into a better mood as we dined. Honestly, I hadn't thought my marriage would matter to her. After all, the whole city had labeled me an adulterer, so my wife wouldn't expect fidelity. Why, then, should I stop seeing Rose?

*It goes against all my principles—and* yours.

Principles didn't matter when it came to Rose. Our arrangement suited us both and we were ridiculously compatible in bed. My marriage wouldn't affect the time I spent with her or my unquenchable desire for her.

I had no intention of giving her up. I merely had to convince her.

"When will we return to New York?" Rose moved the blueberry trifle around on her plate as if she found it distasteful, rather than her favorite dessert. I'd asked the crew to make it specifically for her.

"In four or five days."

"I'd like to return immediately."

A pang of disappointment went through me. "I know you're angry with me, but please, Rose. Let's not cut our holiday short."

"It's nothing to do with that. But I might miss Mr. Martin's decision on the part if I'm not around. It's imperative for me to find work."

I set my knife and fork down carefully, then excused the lone crew member overseeing our meal. When we were alone, I said, "If and when we part, you know I'll settle a large sum on you. Stocks, jewelry, cash . . . whatever you wish. You needn't ever work."

"While I appreciate the generous offer, I've told you many times that I don't need those things from you." She picked up her champagne. "I'm perfectly capable of going back to work."

"Nevertheless, you're getting a large sum of money from me."

A flash of anger lit her gaze before it quickly disappeared. She took a sip of her champagne, then set the glass down. "Let's not quarrel. I don't wish to ruin our time together on the yacht."

"Neither do I." I reached into the pocket of my jacket. "Close your eyes."

She cocked her head, like she didn't know what to make of the request. If we were on better terms, perhaps she might think this was a naughty game. Instead, I merely wanted to surprise her.

"Please," I added.

When she complied, I pulled a large box out of my coat pocket. Then I set it beside her place setting. "Now, open them."

Her lashes fluttered and her gaze immediately found the light blue box. She sat perfectly still for a long minute, her eyes locked on the present. I couldn't tell what she was thinking, so I explained, "I thought of you when I saw this. I hope you like it."

"Moore." She shook her head. "Is this because we argued?"

"No, not unless Mr. Tiffany has opened a store somewhere on my yacht. I bought this beforehand and always planned to give it to you on the boat."

"You needn't give me presents."

"I like to. And I hope it'll make you smile once you finally open the damn thing and see it."

Frowning, she did as I asked. Her fingers soon revealed a long triple strand pearl necklace. A gold clasp with a large emerald held the strands together. "Oh, my God. *Moore*." She lifted the pearls like they were the most precious thing she'd ever seen. "It's beautiful."

"Here." I took the necklace from her fingers and stood up. "Let me put it on."

"Now?"

"Yes, now." Moving behind her chair, I draped the strands around her neck, then fashioned the clasp closed. "There. How do you like it?"

She angled toward me, her smile familiar. It was soft and sweet, exactly like the Rose I knew intimately. Admittedly, I'd purchased this necklace in the hopes of lessening the sting over my pending nuptials, but I did like to spoil her. And I'd keep doing it, if only the stubborn woman would let me.

"I adore it, Moore. But this must've cost a fortune."

It had cost a pretty penny, but she was worth every cent. I dragged one of the strands across her lips. "It looks positively decadent on you."

Grabbing my lapels, she pulled me toward her mouth for a long kiss. Her fingers caressed my jaw, her tongue darting out to twine with mine. "Thank you," she finally whispered.

"I merely wish to make you happy."

Though it was true, I wasn't sure she believed me. How else to explain the sadness that flashed in her gaze before she closed her eyes and kissed me again?

When we broke apart, I pressed my forehead to hers. "Are you still angry with me?"

"I'm not angry, Moore. Indeed, I'm grateful. Your news has reminded me of who I am, my purpose in life."

My stomach hollowed out and I decided I had better sit down. Once I was in my chair, I asked, "What does that mean?"

"It doesn't matter."

My words from earlier today, now thrown back at me. "It matters a great deal. I'd like to hear it, if you please."

"This." She waved her hand, gesturing to the yacht. "It's surreal, like a fairy tale. But it isn't mine. I don't belong here. I'm an actress. Soon I'll be starring on Broadway, my name on the marquee, more famous than Barrymore and Bernhardt. That is what I must focus on."

"You do belong here," I gritted out, irrationally angry at her declaration. "You belong with me."

"No, I don't. Another woman will soon have that right."

Was she going to throw this in my face during each disagreement? "I will never feel for her what I feel for you."

"You might someday. You must give your marriage a chance, Moore."

"A chance for, what? I don't know her and she's far too young for me. She even said I'm too old for her. There is no chance this ends happily, Rose."

"How old is she?"

I realized what I'd done much too late. But I wouldn't lie. The truth would appear in the paper this week. "Nineteen."

The word dropped between us like a stone and Rose's expression wiped clean. She was hiding her reaction from me, something she'd started doing quite a bit. I didn't like it. "Rose—"

"She's exactly my age. What a coincidence." Her voice was calm, measured, giving nothing away.

"It *is* a dashed coincidence. I hope you don't think . . . " Straightening, I said forcefully, "I am not out fishing the theaters and dance halls for young girls to bed. I always assumed you were older."

"It doesn't matter," she repeated—and my muscles tightened in irritation.

"It clearly does matter to you. God, Rose. I'd prefer to have you shout and throw something at me, rather than give me such watered-down reactions. I want your honesty."

"No, you don't," she snapped, her green eyes darkening as she narrowed them on me. "You want my acquiescence. You think your money and position give you the authority to make decisions for me, for both of us. You aren't considering how I feel about this at all. Your sole concern is for yourself, to ensure that your toy isn't taken away from you."

My chest burned, both with outrage and offense. "You make me sound like a spoiled child."

She said nothing, merely stared at me as she sipped from her coupe, those perfect lips kissing the glass rim in silent confirmation.

Through sheer force of will, I calmed my racing heart and cooled my blood. The news of my marriage was still fresh and neither of us were dealing with it well. Lashing out at one another achieved nothing. "You are not my toy," I said steadily. "As I have said, I hold you in the highest esteem. I am . . . besotted. And I don't wish to lose you."

Her expression softened and she reached for my hand. Delicate fingers wound around mine and simply held on. "I don't want to lose you, either. But life often doesn't care what we want. You live in a world where your choices are not your own. I don't pretend to understand it, but there it is. Therefore, we should both admit what we have is nice, but temporary, and enjoy the time we have left."

A darkness settled in my throat, a lump of misery I hadn't experienced since the end of my first marriage. I hated this. I hated that I couldn't convince Rose to stay with me beyond September. I stared at our joined hands and tried not to throw my wineglass across the room.

"Say something," she urged softly.

What was there to say? We were at an impasse, one I'd created. I hadn't wanted any of this, but the wheels were in motion, the unavoidable conclusion swiftly approaching.

Lifting Rose's hand to my lips, I kissed the back of it. "Incidentally, I take very good care of my toys."

She laughed, the sound lightening the air in the room. The knot inside me loosened ever so slightly. Such was this woman's power over me.

Not letting go of my hand, she stood and moved to my side. The fingers on her free hand pulled at my arm. "Let's go down below so that you may prove it."

# Seventeen

Rose

I CLIMBED off the streetcar and stepped onto the walk. The air was frigid today, a cold that matched the ice in my heart.

Moore's engagement party was tomorrow.

The betrothal notice had appeared in the paper earlier this week, a whole half page in the *New York World*. The story only garnered a mere two paragraphs in *The New York Times*, but the *World* had included illustrations of the happy couple. I hadn't been able to keep from obsessing over it, reading every word twice and studying the drawings. The writer didn't mention Moore's former marriage, which no doubt had been a demand from the powerful Emerson family. It wouldn't do to bring up past unpleasantness and soil the happy occasion.

Miss Whitney-Dunn was perfectly pretty and descended from a venerable Knickerbocker family. She was everything Moore required in a bride, and I hadn't allowed myself to cry. A woman such as me, temporary and fleeting, a lowly actress, was a diversion for a man like Moore. His legacy required a woman of substance and breeding, and Gladys certainly fit that mold.

I tried to be happy for him.

He was extra attentive the night after the notice was published, and I wasn't certain if the reassurance was for me or him. We didn't speak of it, but he had to know I had seen the newspapers. And if I clung to him a bit tighter as we slept, he hadn't seemed to mind.

Why had I allowed myself to fall in love with him? The age-old question. I wasn't the first woman to ask it, and I certainly wouldn't be the last.

I hurried to Mr. Martin's office. He'd sent word this morning that he had news. Which was good, because I had news for him.

The streets were mostly empty, with New Yorkers preferring to stay someplace warm on such a cold day. I couldn't blame them. I was very much looking forward to returning to the town house and sitting in front of the fire.

After I announced myself to the secretary, I sat to wait in the ante-room. Mr. Martin came out a few moments later, his expression full of excitement when he spotted me. "Rose! Come in, come in. Thank you for coming uptown to see me."

*Downtown,* I considered correcting. But then I would need to explain where I was living and why, hardly a conversation I wished to have with my former director.

"Of course," I said as I lowered myself into a chair. "It's nice to see you again."

"And you." He studied me. "Though I must say, you're looking tired. Is anything amiss?"

Never words a woman liked to hear. "I'm perfectly well. A late night, is all."

"Well," he said, rubbing his hands together. "You had best get all the sleep you can before September. Guess who has been chosen as the lead in *The Bathing Girl*?"

I couldn't prevent a burst of happiness from blooming in my chest. *I got the part!* Me, not Sarah Bernhardt. If I'd ever doubted my abilities, this was validation of my talent. I could find work as a lead actress, damn it.

Drawing in a deep breath, I let it out slowly. "Thank you very much, Mr. Martin. I'm afraid I must decline, however."

His face fell dramatically. "I beg your pardon. Decline?"

"I'm grateful for the opportunity, but I cannot accept it."

"Why the devil not? This could be the role of a lifetime, Rose. Think about what you are saying."

Oh, I had thought about it. A lot.

And I couldn't stay in New York. It held too many memories, too much temptation. Thankfully, the deed to the town house meant I had the means to go *anywhere*. As soon as I sold the property, I could travel to Paris and perform there. Or London. Rome. A place where they didn't know the Emersons and I wouldn't need to hear of Moore's wedding.

I'd moved cities before, so I knew how to find work and lodgings. Make friends and build a life. It wouldn't be difficult—once my heart mended, of course.

There wasn't a choice. Under no circumstance could I stay in New York and watch Moore and Gladys's family grow. And did I honestly think I could resist an overture from Moore after he married? I was strong, but my love for him weakened me. If he approached me and pressed, would my principles outlast my longing for him?

I didn't wish to find out.

I gave Mr. Martin my best imitation of a smile. "I know it sounds strange, but I plan to move abroad. Europe, maybe."

He stroked his chin, his gaze thoughtful. "I can think of only a few reasons why a rising theatrical celebrity like yourself would travel abroad instead of taking this role. Are you . . .?" He gestured to my middle.

My eyes rounded. "No, I'm not. It isn't that."

"So it must be a man. Allow me to guess? He's convincing you to follow him overseas. Put your dreams on hold to cater to his traveling whims."

That hit a little too close to the truth and the backs of my eyelids began to sting. I could feel the tears gathering, a lump settling in my throat. "No, that isn't the case. I'm doing this alone."

When a tear slipped free and worked its way down my cheek, Mr. Martin paled and quickly handed me his handkerchief. "Oh, Rose. Forgive me. It's none of my business why you're leaving."

I dabbed at my face. "Your shock is understandable. I'm a little surprised myself, to be honest. And you'll never know how sorry I am to turn down this role."

"Then don't do it. We won't start rehearsals until April. Go and travel all you like, then return refreshed and ready to work."

He didn't understand. It wasn't my present circumstances that worried me. It was what happened in September and beyond that I couldn't handle. "I'm afraid leaving now won't help. I'm sorry, but I can't give you additional details."

Shaking his head, he stood and thrust his hands in his pockets. "You'll be hard to replace, Rose. The producers thought you were just the perfect girl for the role."

"I'm honored to be considered, truly. And I'm certain it'll be a smash."

He cocked his head and considered me. Then he said, "I'll sit on this for a week. In case you change your mind."

I didn't argue, though I knew I wouldn't change my mind. "Thank you, Mr. Martin. For all you've done for me."

We said our goodbyes and I left, my stomach heavy. Yet I knew this was the right decision. The future had a lot in store for Rose O'Don-ahue . . . just not here in New York.

# Eighteen

Moore

I TUGGED ON MY COLLAR. The receiving line at the betrothal ball stretched down the stairs and through the entry hall, an endless stream of guests to congratulate the happy couple.

Never mind that neither the bride nor the bridegroom appeared very happy. In fact, I'd say we both looked downright miserable. The only people wearing smiles tonight were my mother and Gladys's father.

"Welcome to the family, son," Whitney-Dunn had said earlier, even though he wasn't old enough to be my father. I'd barely restrained myself from punching him.

As for my mother, I was glad to see her in such good spirits. Ever since I informed her of my decision to marry, my mother had been cheerful, showing a renewed vigor for anything wedding-related. To prevent my mother from overtaxing herself, I asked our housekeeper to hire an army of additional servants to deal with tonight's ball. With Louis Sherry overseeing the food, my mother hadn't worried over a single detail.

"Congratulations, Mr. Emerson," an older gentleman was saying as we shook hands.

"Thank you. It is nice to see you. Enjoy your evening." I'd repeated the same thing over and over since the doors opened. I was fucking exhausted.

*I wish Rose were here.*

If she were standing beside me right now, I wouldn't feel as though a dark cloud hung over my head. Like I was headed to the gallows, not the altar.

The next man stepped in front of me and thrust out his hand stiffly. "Congratulations, Emerson."

I knew him from the clubs around town, which didn't explain why he sounded surly. No one had reason for bitterness here save me. "Hyde, good evening."

Silent, Charles Hyde moved on to Gladys, where he nodded briefly and kept going without a word. I frowned. That was odd. I didn't remember Hyde being so rude in years past.

A different face appeared and the pleasantries continued. I kissed hands, shook palms, and tried not to bolt. It wasn't easy to stand still in the face of my worst nightmare.

When we finally ended, I longed to walk out the front door and never return. A headache pounded behind my eyes. "I'll return in a bit," I told my mother. "There's some work I must attend to."

"Oh, Moore," my mother said, holding onto my arm. "Really. Can it not wait? There are toasts to give and the two of you must dance."

I bent to kiss her cheek and peeled her fingers from my wool coat. "Later, please." After a polite nod to Gladys—and ignoring Whitney-Dunn altogether—I strode to my office and closed the door.

Blessed silence.

The bourbon and solitude in my private space were like a balm for my ragged soul. I sat at my desk and dug into the notes and files left behind by my assistants. It was a familiar routine. Work has been my refuge for the last eight years. Until Rose came along, of course. But after September, I wouldn't have her any longer.

I pushed that depressing thought away and concentrated on my reports.

I lost track of time. When I finally looked up, an hour and a half had disappeared along with a good portion of bourbon. No doubt my mother was pulling her hair out, wondering where I was. The weight atop my shoulders increased, the pressure of my unwanted future like a boulder above my head.

*Stop complaining. You have no choice.*

Rising, I grabbed a pen and dashed off a quick note to Rose, saying I'd visit as quickly as I could manage tonight. No matter the late hour, I needed to see her.

Carrying the note, I left the office to find a footman. Hopefully, he could get the note over to Rose's town house before she went to bed. Unfortunately, the corridor was empty, not a footman in sight. I considered going into the ballroom to summon one, but I had a deep-seated aversion to encountering any guests at the moment.

Then I realized one of the grooms could perform this errand. Decision made, I skulked like a thief through the connected interior rooms, my feet silent on the plush carpets. I kept going, room by empty room, thinking of all the ways I would defile Rose's delectable body tonight.

When I walked into the library, I heard a gasp and the rustle of skirts.

*What on earth?*

I turned toward the sound and discovered two figures standing close together near the windows. It was Gladys . . . and Hyde. Guilt was written all over her face, not to mention that her lips were swollen. Like they'd recently been kissed.

I stared, unsure what to say. This was certainly unexpected. Gladys hadn't struck me as particularly amorous or adventurous, yet she'd been miserable at the prospect of marrying me. Was this because of Hyde?

They both watched me warily, as if I might attack at any moment. Most men, I supposed, would be quite angry in this situation. Not me. If anything, this made my life easier. At least Rose would now believe that infidelity posed no problem in my marriage.

Let Gladys have Hyde. I would keep Rose and we'd all feign innocence in public.

"Excuse me," I said with a polite nod in my fiancée's direction as I started across the room.

"Moore, wait," Gladys blurted behind me.

I paused at the door. "Yes?"

She exchanged a look with Hyde. "Tell him," Gladys said, nudging her lover's arm.

Hyde drew himself up, though his cheeks were red. "Moore, you should know that Gladys and I are in love."

Did they believe this mattered? Love didn't factor into our marriage. "And?"

That threw them off. The two exchanged another uncertain glance before Gladys said, "Charles and I have been trying to think of a way to break the engagement. Except, as you know, my father is dead set on the match."

"I'm aware," I grumbled and grabbed the latch to leave.

Gladys's voice once again stopped me. "Moore, wait. Where are you going?"

I sighed in exasperation. "To find a groom. Following that, I'll circulate in the ballroom and dance with you. Then I plan to go and visit my mistress."

"A mistress?"

"Yes—and I don't plan on giving her up after the wedding."

Gladys cocked her head. "You love her."

A denial sprang to my lips, but the words wouldn't come. Did I love Rose? I hadn't experienced the emotion before. Hadn't thought myself capable of it, honestly. Wasn't love soft and sweet, a rainbow of happiness and sunshine?

Such were not my feelings for Rose.

Instead, I felt fevered and frenzied, like I would go mad without her. A caged beast, angry at anyone and anything that kept me from her side. She turned me into a selfish and demanding version of myself, one I hardly recognized.

Was this love? Doubtful. Obsession? Most definitely.

"It doesn't matter," I told the couple across the room. "Now, if you'll both excuse me."

"Wait!" Gladys exclaimed. "Why do you still plan to marry me, even though our hearts have been given to others?"

Was she truly so young, so naive? "Be serious, Gladys. Marriage in our world has naught to do with hearts."

"It's not too late, Emerson," Hyde said. "The vows have not yet been recited."

I folded my arms, leaned against the door, and shook my head. "There is no breaking this off. I suggest you both put it out of your mind."

"Why? I refuse to accept my fate." She lifted her chin. "I would like to think you had the same backbone."

Now she was insulting me? My jaw tight, I pointed in the direction of the ballroom. "There are two hundred people out there celebrating this union. It's appeared in the newspapers. I won't cause another scandal by breaking off this engagement, so you'd best brace yourself to go through with it."

"But . . . " She glanced at Hyde, a silent conversation passing between them.

"Be reasonable, Moore," Hyde said after a beat. "Let us arrive at a solution that benefits everyone."

"Benefits you, you mean." I put my hands on my hips, contemplating what a broken engagement would do to my mother. This could very well kill her. "I don't want this marriage, but it is happening. You two are free to continue your affair both before and after the ceremony. God knows I will try to do the same with Mrs. O'Donahue. All I ask is that my children are my own."

Gladys paled, her discomfort visible. "I cannot believe you are so willing to throw away your future."

I gnashed my back teeth together, the grinding sound echoing in my ears. "You are young and foolish if you believe either of us has a choice in this. And crying off will only cause a scandal. Believe me when I tell you, there will be no scandal."

"Any public spectacle would be short-lived," Gladys tried.

My voice rose in volume as my frustration bubbled over. "It doesn't matter! A public spectacle might very well kill my mother and cost me control of the company!"

Gladys frowned and reached to clasp Hyde's hand. "Are you being blackmailed into marrying me?"

The door opened, startling all of us. I looked over and saw my mother enter the library. "What on earth is happening in here? I heard raised—"

She froze when she saw Gladys holding Hyde's hand. Then my mother glanced at me, her forehead lined with concern. "Oh, dear."

Immediately, I started for her side, worried this might affect her health. "It's nothing to worry about, mother. We're sorting out a few things before the ceremony. Why don't you return to the ballroom?"

"Stop coddling me. You've been treating me like an invalid since the engagement was announced." She shot a disapproving look at Gladys, then hissed, "Have you no shame, Miss Whitney-Dunn? We are at your betrothal ball."

Whitney-Dunn strode into the room "Charlotte, I've been looking —" He stopped in his tracks, taking in the scene. Gladys had dropped Hyde's hand, but she hadn't moved away from the young man's side. "What the devil is going on in here?"

Hyde took a step forward. "I'd like to marry your daughter, sir."

"Over my dead body," Whitney-Dunn snapped, throwing the door closed behind him. "Gladys, get in the damn ballroom with your fiancé right now."

Gladys came forward and wrapped a hand around Hyde's arm. "Father, I want to marry Charles."

"I don't care what you want," her father said. "You'll do as you're told. And you will be marrying Emerson in September."

"No, I won't. I'll run away and elope before I marry another man."

"We discussed this," Whitney-Dunn practically growled. "I want you married to Emerson, not this penniless nobody." He gestured to Hyde.

"Wait," my mother said, her voice patient but confused. "You knew of this association, Harold? Yet you allowed my son to propose to her anyway?"

*Allowed me* to propose? I almost snorted.

Whitney-Dunn had the grace to appear contrite. "Now, Charlotte. This is nothing for you to worry about. I'll straighten out this situation. Gladys will make an excellent wife to your son."

"Not if she's allowed another man to take her virtue and claim her heart. I wouldn't wish for Moore to be dishonored in such a way."

Whitney-Dunn's face began to turn red. "She is virtuous. Hyde has clearly been filling her head with nonsense, but I'll put a stop to it right away."

I could see my mother's chest rising and falling, her breathing picking up as her face paled. A knot of fear tightened in my belly. "Mother, why don't you sit down? I wouldn't want your heart to act up again."

Her head swung toward me, her brows lowered into a deep groove. "My heart? There's nothing wrong with my heart." Her expression cleared. "Is this why you've been asking after my health every day?"

I held up my palms in apology. "I've spoken with Dr. Fritz. It's all right. I know about your condition."

"Condition? I don't have a condition. I saw Dr. Fritz six weeks ago and he gave me a clean bill of health."

That made no sense. "Are you certain? Because Whitney-Dunn and Dr. Fritz confirmed your heart condition. You're supposed to avoid any undue strain whatsoever."

My mother drew herself up and faced Whitney-Dunn, her body vibrating with visible anger. "I think we'd all best sit down. Harold, I believe you owe me an explanation."

# Nineteen

Rose

**"GOOD MORNING, DARLING."**

The fog of sleep evaporated slowly as I came awake. I blinked, my eyes filling with the dull gray light clinging to the windows. Raindrops pinged quietly against the glass. I was surprised to find Moore already dressed and perched on the edge of my bed. Normally, he departed for work and didn't wake me.

I licked my lips to moisten them. "What time is it?"

"A little after eight. I had them bring up breakfast for us." Rising, he placed a tray on the bed next to me, then sat again. "I have news."

Sakes alive, this man. He'd arrived in the middle of the night in an energetic state, almost manic. After rousing me from sleep, he'd taken me fast and hard, wringing orgasms from my body as if someone were keeping score. Subsequently, every part of me was sore today.

But worse than my aching body was my aching heart. I couldn't handle any additional revelations. The engagement news had nearly broken me.

"I need coffee first." I pushed up to a sitting position. While I was settling on my pillows, he poured a cup of coffee and dropped a lump of sugar in it as I preferred. "Thank you," I said as he handed the cup and saucer to me.

I took a grateful sip and ignored the expectant, eager look on Moore's face. There hadn't been time in the middle of the night to talk. Instead, I'd been demanding of his body, shameless and insatiable. Almost as if I were saying goodbye.

*You will be soon.*

I shook off my melancholy. This was the cold light of day and the truth couldn't hide. "What is it?"

"It's about my betrothal party."

My stomach clenched so violently that I wondered if I might throw up. Did he think I was interested in the ice sculptures and party favors? I set my cup and saucer down on the nightstand. "Moore—"

"I know it's not your favorite topic, but I swear you'll want to hear this."

"Fine." I clasped my fingers together and wiped the emotion from my face. "And how was the party? Well attended, I hope."

"Don't do that. Not with me." He put his hand on my thigh, squeezing.

"I haven't a clue as to what you mean."

"Yes, you do." Bending over the tray, he kissed me briefly on the mouth. "You show me a glimpse of your real feelings, but they quickly disappear behind a mask of indifference. I don't want the actress. I want *you*, Rose."

No, he didn't. He wanted the perfect mistress who provided him the perfect respite. Someone who wouldn't complain about his infidelity and distract him from the tedium in his life. I wasn't allowed to have thoughts and feelings and opinions. Why would I, when all he wanted was my body? Some other woman would get his name, his home. His children and his future.

I rubbed my forehead and tried to focus. It was far too early in the day for such sad reflections. "Moore, perhaps I should get dressed for this conversation. I'm not feeling myself."

"Another moment, please. Hear me out."

"As long as it's quick."

"It is. So I was drinking bourbon and working—"

"*During* your engagement party?"

His eyebrows dipped low, annoyed at my interruption. "I thought we covered that bit already."

What was this, a Feydeau farce play? "I'm surprised you weren't with your fiancée."

"You'll understand in a moment, I promise. So here I am, working and drinking and missing you. I decided to send you a note to let you know that I'd be paying a visit after the party."

I hadn't received any message. Still, I waved my hand for him to continue.

"Because I'm hiding from the guests," he said, "I must travel through the interior rooms rather than the corridor. I'm creeping through my own home like a damn thief when I come across a couple embracing in the library." He paused. "It was Gladys and another man."

I sucked air into my lungs. "*What?*" How could she possibly be so stupid? This woman had *Moore* and she was with another man. Was she cracked?

"Settle down." He patted my leg. "This gets better. Turns out she and this other man are in love."

"She tells you this at your engagement party? And people think *I* have a flair for the dramatic? Good lord."

"I didn't mind. Better to learn it now than after our wedding."

"You weren't mad that she was with another man?"

"Absolutely not. As I told you more than once, there are no feelings between us. In fact, I was glad. I thought it might help illustrate that you needn't worry about infidelity."

My hands curled into fists. Unbelievable, this man. "Moore, this doesn't change anyth—"

He tossed a newspaper on my lap. "Read it."

I tore my angry gaze off his face to see the black and white print. The headline couldn't be missed.

*WHITNEY-DUNN HEIRESS THROWS OVER EMERSON, WEDS HYDE*

"Throws over?"

He reached for a piece of toast and took a large bite. "Keep reading, darling."

As I read, my eyes grew wider and wider. It turned out that Gladys and a Mr. Charles Hyde had disappeared from the betrothal ball sometime around eleven o'clock, traveling to New Jersey to elope. "This is unbelievable."

"Incidentally, I'm buying them a boat as a wedding present."

"You're happy about this? Won't the gossips attack your family?"

"Perhaps, but I no longer care. Whitney-Dunn lied to me, said my mother had a heart condition to force me into the marriage with his daughter. He wanted to get a foothold into my company and knew marriage was the best way to do it. But when my mother learned of what he'd done, she demanded to call off the betrothal, even with all those guests there." The edge of his mouth kicked up. "She put Whitney-Dunn in his place. Then I kicked him off the Emerson Board. It was utterly glorious."

Ah, so these had been the circumstances he spoke of, the ones he hadn't wished to share with me. "Congratulations," I told him. "I'm happy for you."

He put down his half-eaten toast and dusted off his hands. "Darling, I'm happy for *us*. Can you not see what this means for our future together? I can give you everything you've ever wanted."

*Our future together.*

*Everything you've ever wanted.*

Hope took flight in my chest like a thousand butterflies. Goodness. Was he saying that we would . . . ? Were my feelings for him returned? I swallowed. Moore *loved* me. He wanted marriage and a home. Perhaps children one day.

*I am besotted. And I don't wish to lose you.*

He truly meant it.

I grabbed his arm, needing to touch him. "Oh, Moore."

He nodded encouragingly. "Exactly. It means nothing changes." Leaning over on an elbow, he worked his free hand under the bedclothes. Clever fingers crept along my bare thigh. "We continue just as if this wedding business never happened."

*Oh.* Oh.

My heart shriveled in my chest.

I was so stupid. He didn't want me for a *wife*. He wanted to keep me in this town house, ready and available for whenever he wished. A paid companion to fuck him until the day he tired of me.

*Stupid, stupid Rose.*

How dare I dream of a position to which I had no right, a life that would never be mine? I knew better. I would never be acceptable in this man's eyes. For a bed partner, yes—but never for a wife. Exactly like Tommy.

Tears stung the back of my eyelids. Why was I never good enough? No, I hadn't been born of Dutch descent or to a wealthy family. But I was a good, caring person with decent morals and intelligence. So when would these selfish men stop breaking my heart?

I couldn't do this any longer. I'd planned to leave the country in September, but I needed to go *now*. I needed to get far away from this man.

Suddenly, Moore filled my vision, his large hands gripping my face. "What's wrong? Christ, Rose. I thought you would be thrilled about this. Please, tell me what I've said."

My cheeks were wet. I hadn't realized I was crying. "You should go."

"No, sweetheart." He pressed his lips to my forehead. "Tell me what has upset you. Please."

For some reason, that made me cry harder. I hated him at that moment. Every poem and play and story had lied to me about love. Being in love was awful and terrible, a wretched state of existence. It clawed away your insides, taking and taking, until you had nothing left to give. It left you a hollow shell of a person.

Moore pulled me into his chest. "Oh, my gorgeous girl. Let me help. Let me make it better."

All I could think was, *Love me. Keep me. Don't ever let me go.*

But he couldn't promise those things. No man from his world could, not to a woman like me.

And maybe it was time for the truth. I was tired of hiding my feelings from him. If he knew, then he would let me go.

I eased back so he could see the destruction on my face. "I'm crying because for a brief second I thought you were about to propose to me."

His face slackened in absolute shock and horror. I would've laughed under any other circumstance. But the fact that it hadn't even occurred to him was why this would never work. His eyebrows lowered as he frowned. "Rose—"

"Please, don't." I didn't want to hear his explanation. "I know better, I promise. But I've fallen in love with you and for a split second, I forgot."

He blinked slowly, his brow wrinkling in confusion. "Forgot?"

"I forgot that you're you and I'm me. That our worlds couldn't be further apart." I eased out of the bed, desperate to put space between us. "I think you should go."

"Wait, please. I need a moment to catch up, Rose."

"There's nothing to discuss. And I cannot keep doing this with you."

"What does that mean?"

I clasped my arms around my middle and struggled to remain calm. "Did you not hear me? I've fallen in love with you. I've been a wreck because you were marrying someone else!"

"But I'm not marrying her anymore."

"There will be another Gladys. If not tomorrow, then next month or next year. You aren't mine to keep. You'll marry some other woman and my heart will break all over again. I can't go through it. It's too painful."

He dragged a hand down his face. "I'm not going to remarry. I promise."

"I don't believe you, especially when you've already broken your word to me. And it doesn't even matter! I deserve to be enough for someone. I deserve to be a wife, to be walked down an aisle and have vows spoken before God. I will always want more than you are willing to give—and it will slowly destroy me over time to have it withheld."

"Please. Let's give it time."

"I cannot. I cannot keep hiding my true feelings for you, burying them because I don't wish to upset you. I'm tired of playing the part of your mistress and acting like I don't want all of you. Because I do and it's killing me inside."

His jaw went as stiff as granite. "I don't want you playing a part with me. I want you, Rose, plain and simple."

"No, you want a fun and easy lover, undemanding of your time or affection. She gives everything and asks for nothing in return."

"That's unfair. You haven't asked for anything before now. This is the first I'm hearing of marriage. You've surprised me, is all."

Surprised him, because the possibility never occurred to him. God, I was pathetic. Trying to appear casual, I waved my hand. "It doesn't matter. I'd planned to leave New York after you married. I'll move up my plans and depart immediately."

He slapped a hand on the mattress. "Damn it, Rose. You cannot leave New York. I won't allow it!"

"You'll not allow it?" I gaped at him, then let out a joyless laugh. "You have no authority over my life, Moore. None whatsoever. Our arrangement is over."

"Don't say that. We aren't finished."

I was too furious and hurt to look at him. I stared at the wall, wishing I'd never snuck into his carriage all those months ago. I wish I'd never met Alfred Moore Emerson III. "Please, go."

"I can't believe you're throwing away what we have. I think I love you."

"You *think*?" My voice rose comically. Convenient he was telling me now, when I was ready to walk out of his life. My god, this man's selfishness knew no bounds. I pointed to the door. "Get out."

He dragged both of his hands through his hair. "Rose, for fuck's sake. Give me a second to think. All of this has thrown me sideways."

"That isn't my concern. Go and think somewhere else. I need to be away from you."

"As long as you promise you won't leave New York. Promise me you'll stay and we can try to work this out."

He wasn't listening to me. He was still trying to bend me to his will, to get what he wanted. My wishes and desires, other than what happened in bed, mattered little to him. My heart ached at the idea of losing him, of never seeing him again, but my head had decided this was over.

I stared at Moore for the last time, my handsome uptown prince.

Maybe in another life this third act wouldn't end so tragically. We could've married and lived happily ever after.

But this was reality, not a Broadway play.

Actresses didn't mix with the Knickerbocker elites unless they were being paid for the privilege, and the gilded compensation wasn't worth the heartache. *I* was worth more. And I was done letting a man have control over me and my future. It was time to stand on my own once again.

However, I knew him. He would try to find me and his money meant he had resources to spare. So I had to do this carefully. I needed to leave quickly and never look back, begin a life someplace without Astors and Vanderbilts and Emersons.

But I would survive. It was what women like me did.

I gave him a bland look. "I won't leave yet. We may discuss this tomorrow. For now, please give me space."

He didn't move for a long moment. Then he snagged his coat off the chair back, shrugged it on, and came toward me. "Good. This isn't finished, Rose. We'll talk later." He kissed my forehead, then strode into the hall.

I listened to his footsteps recede, then I heard the front door close with a snap. I bit my lip, trying to stem the tears as best I could, the pain worse than I could've imagined.

But I would hold firm. He and I were most definitely finished.

# Twenty

Moore

"FORGIVE ME, Mr. Emerson, but there's been no trace."

My fingers curled around the edges of my desk so that I didn't throw something. Or someone. "You aren't looking carefully enough. A woman like Miss O'Donahue does not just *disappear*. Find. Her," I growled.

The Pinkerton detective held up his palms. "Sir, we have fifteen detectives out twelve hours a day searching for her."

I slammed my palm on the wooden desktop. "Then hire fifteen more and work twenty hours a day!" I didn't care what it cost or who I had to badger. Rose disappeared three weeks ago and I needed answers. "She is somewhere and I need you all to find her."

"We've checked all the places you suggested and we've spoken with everyone who knows her. She didn't buy a rail or steamer ticket, and she didn't board a coach." He shrugged. "We are out of ideas."

As was I. I'd been out every day, every night, searching. Talking to anyone with even a brief association with Rose. They all claimed ignorance, even when I badgered them. No one knew her whereabouts, or at least they weren't telling anyone if they did.

I was losing my fucking mind.

The fury and panic gathering beneath my skin burst free, my rage choking me. Picking up the crystal tumbler on my desk, I hurled it against the wall. It didn't lessen my anger in the least, so I grabbed another tumbler and hurled that one, too. "Get out! You're fired!" I shouted at the Pinkerton. "You and the rest of the detectives are all fired. I'll find her my-goddamn-self!"

My office door opened and my mother's voice filled the room. "What in heaven's name is happening in here?"

"Everything is fine. This gentleman was just leaving." I waved my hand and rubbed my tired eyes. "No need for concern."

The Pinkerton dashed out of my office, the coward. My mother, on the other hand, didn't budge. Ignoring her, I picked up the report on Rose's last-known whereabouts—from two weeks ago—and began reading it again.

After a beat of silence, I heard the door close. Skirts rustled as footsteps sounded on the carpet. "This isn't a good time," I told her. "Whatever it is will need to wait."

"This will not wait. Furthermore, I am your mother and I will not tolerate such disrespect. Now, pull your head out of your arse and address me properly."

Never in all my thirty-eight years had I heard my mother use a crude word.

My jaw fell open as my head snapped up.

"I see I have your attention." She lowered herself into the chair the Pinkerton had vacated. "Good. Now, this has gone on long enough. You've been worse than a wounded bear since the engagement ended, which I find thoroughly confusing. I would think you'd be pleased to remain a bachelor. So why are you throwing my best crystal and terrorizing Pinkertons?"

I couldn't tell her. She wouldn't understand or approve. "It's nothing for you to worry about."

"Is this about Miss O'Donahue?"

All the air left my lungs in a rush. "How do you know her name?"

"Moore." She sighed. "I may be getting up in years, but do you honestly think I'm unaware of your association with her? Rumblings have reached my ears for weeks now. As we both know, Fifth Avenue is a very small world. And Miss O'Donahue is a talented actress and quite beautiful, from what I understand."

The damn gossips. I couldn't ever escape. "I suppose this was why you pushed for me to marry Gladys."

"Let me be clear: I wanted you to marry, plain and simple. I still do. But when Harold suggested his daughter, I couldn't see a reason to refuse. Of course, no one knew she was embroiled in an affair with Mr. Hyde, but that's a discussion for another day. You need a woman to soften your edges, Moore. To help you see there's more to life than sitting behind a desk."

Rose had done that. She'd gifted me with more joy than I ever dreamed possible.

*I deserve to be enough for someone.*

She *was* enough for me. Rose was all I ever needed—and when I found her again I would make sure she never doubted it.

"You've hired Pinkertons to find someone, so am I to understand that Miss O'Donahue has left New York?"

I was too exhausted to lie. "Yes. She is very angry with me."

"Why? What did you do?"

"She confessed that she loved me and wished to marry. Except I bungled it. I . . . didn't know what to say. It took me by surprise."

"Understandable, considering men of your station do not marry actresses."

I'd thought about this a lot while the Pinkertons were searching for Rose. Because if—no, *when*—I found her I was giving Rose everything she wanted. I didn't care what it was, because I wouldn't lose her again. "George Gould married Edith Kingdon. The two are quite happy, in fact."

My mother wrinkled her nose. "Well, the *Goulds*. What does one expect from that family?"

"Disparage them if you like, but times are changing, mother. And we'd best change with them. I married Eugenia out of duty and lived to regret it. God knows I would've been miserable married to Gladys. I'm not entertaining the possibility ever again. People wish to marry for love."

"Do you love this woman?"

"Yes," I answered immediately. "Unequivocally. And I'm going to marry her."

Her eyes rounded. "What of the talk? The entire city will dine on this news for months and rip you apart as they did before."

"I couldn't care less." And I didn't. As Rose once said, they were just words. What mattered was having the right people stand beside you during the difficult times. "I'm sorry the first scandal killed Papa, more than you'll ever know, but I can't—"

"Killed your father? What on earth?" She leaned forward and placed her hand on the desk, almost as if she were reaching for me. "You cannot truly believe such nonsense, do you?"

I swallowed hard. "We both know he was in perfect health before the divorce trial. He tried to talk me out of it for weeks. Then his heart gave out once . . . " I couldn't manage the rest. My exhaustion and worry and heartache was bringing all of my pain to the surface, making it difficult to speak.

"Oh, Moore. That wasn't what happened. My dear boy, you've blamed yourself all this time." Her eyes grew glassy. "I'm so terribly sorry. I didn't . . . Well, I prefer that you never learn the true circumstances." She drew in a deep breath. "He died in bed with another woman."

The room tunneled to my mother's face and this revelation. Ears ringing, I said, "What?"

She toyed with her pearls, looking as nervous as I'd ever seen. "A mistress. Down on Jane Street. Imagine when she rang our telephone to inform me. I was utterly horrified."

"Were you aware of her?"

"Yes. All men think they are clever at hiding these things, but wives always know. Or at least suspect. Anyway, I have to assume his liaison was one of the reasons he didn't want you to go through with your trial. No doubt he worried the increased attention on the family might reveal his secret."

Reeling, I dragged my hand down my face. "This is unbelievable," I mumbled. "All this time . . . "

"So when Whitney-Dunn told you of my heart troubles, you thought you'd cause my death, as well."

I nodded, not surprised that she'd put it together. "I couldn't bear to be responsible. I couldn't lose you, too."

"Moore, you are not responsible for his death. Put that firmly out of your mind. And if I die, it's my time and no one's fault. Do you hear me? Stop sacrificing your happiness for your parents. It is supposed to be the other way around, for heaven's sake."

It was like a heavy weight lifted off my shoulders. I drew in the first truly deep breath since the trial began all those years ago. "I'm going to marry Rose, mother. Your daughter-in-law will be an actress from Ohio. I suggest you start growing accustomed to the idea."

"I will welcome her because I love you, but not everyone will understand. You must realize the obstacles you'll both face, the gossip and derision."

"Let everyone talk. I won't hide her or our marriage. In fact, to announce the engagement, I'll buy a full page advert in every newspaper from here to—"

My jaw closed with a snap.

The newspapers. Of course. Those rags had once used me to sell copies, ripping me apart in my darkest moment. Perhaps it was time to use *them*.

"What is it?" my mother asked. "I see you've arrived at a conclusion of some sort. Does this mean you've realized where Miss O'Donahue has gone?"

"No, but I may have a way to reach her." I stood and buttoned my topcoat. "If you'll excuse me."

"Grandchildren, Moore. *Legitimate* grandchildren. That is all I ask."

I strode across the Persian carpets, hurrying toward the corridor. "Believe me, I'm working on it."

# Twenty-One

Rose

*Paris*

## IT WAS A FULL-PAGE ADVERT.

I might not have learned of the advert at all, if not for a fellow American actress who offered me congratulations as I arrived at the theater. Seeing my confusion, she produced the morning edition of *Le Figaro*, where I found the advert on page 3. Big block letters spread out on the page to read:

*MR. ALFRED MOORE EMERSON III ANNOUNCES HIS BETROTHAL TO MISS ROSE O'DONAHUE.*

There was a smaller story at the bottom about how the wedding would take place after I returned to New York, as I was currently starring in a traveling theatrical production. My incredulity rose with every letter and sentence.

*Of all the dashed nerve.*

First, I crumpled the newsprint into a tiny ball, then I marched to the nearest *télégraphe* office. Moore had lost his mind, apparently. I never consented to marry him. Furthermore, he hadn't *asked*.

Wasn't this high-handedness exactly like him?

I sent a cable to the *New York World*, asking them to print my response *and* bill it to Moore:

*MISS ROSE O'DONAHUE DELIVERS EMPHATIC REJECTION OF MR. ALFRED MOORE EMERSON III'S PROPOSAL.*

*TALENTED ACTRESS UNINTERESTED IN TYCOON'S SHENANIGANS.*

There. Let him choke on that.

Then I returned to work.

* * *

Two days later another full-page advert appeared:

*MR. ALFRED MOORE EMERSON III BEGS MISS ROSE O'DONAHUE FOR ANOTHER CHANCE.*

*TYCOON DETERMINED TO MARRY FAMOUS ACTRESS.*

I snorted and hid my smile behind a sip of my morning *chocolat*. How was he managing this? By placing adverts in every major newspaper around the globe? The man had money to burn, apparently.

I could only imagine what New York Society thought of these exchanges. The city would likely run out of smelling salts. What happened to his concern over gossip and avoiding a scandal? This was a scandal of Moore's own making.

I stared at the words on the newsprint and my toes curled. I hardly believed they were real. Moore wanted to *marry* me? So what had changed his mind?

I missed him, certainly. And this was flattering. Never would I have believed him capable of such a public display of his feelings.

Still, he'd hurt me.

*I think I love you.*

I rubbed the center of my chest, wishing for the permanent ache lodged there to dissipate. I wanted a partner who loved me beyond reason, without any shred of doubt. So was Moore's stunt about love . . . or about the reacquisition of his favorite toy?

I wasn't certain. And guessing was too great of a risk. If I were wrong, then I ended up precisely back where we started—and I had far too much pride for that.

Paris was my future and there was no reason to dwell in the past. Eventually, I would recover from this heartache and feel happiness like before. One thing I knew for certain? Never again would I agree to being a man's mistress.

I folded the newspaper and set it aside. There was no use in sending a response.

* * *

The adverts appeared like clockwork.

Over the next three weeks *Le Figaro* printed another declaration from Moore every other day. At first it was embarrassing, but the theater where I performed loved the publicity. Tickets were sold out every night, the Parisians racing to see the actress who had an American tycoon chasing after her. I quickly developed into a celebrity, as the French adored love above all things.

Everywhere I went people were full of advice. Most of the men said I should give Moore another chance, while the women thought Moore should suffer. "*Vive la résistance!*" they shouted at me as I walked along the boulevards and during our curtain calls.

Admittedly, the attention was nice. But I wondered when Moore would give up. This couldn't last forever and I hadn't responded, save after the first advert. At some point he would realize his folly and stop trying to convince me.

Would I be relieved? Or devastated? I wasn't certain.

The show in which I performed was unremarkable at best. However, I was grateful they hired me after only a brief audition and a letter from Mr. Martin touting my abilities. The wages allowed me to eat well and sleep with a roof over my head, considering I left New York with almost nothing but the clothes on my back.

"*Allez! Allez!*" the stage manager hissed, waving his hand for all of us to go out on stage. It was the end of another show, another curtain call.

The performers filled the tiny stage and we all bowed, the audience clapping for us. Everyone pushed me forward, and the cheers grew louder, along with shouts of resistance. I blew kisses and soaked in the attention. God, I loved Paris.

When we finished I strode to my dressing room, ready to remove my costume and find my bed. The other actors like to frequent cafés and restaurants, where they would drink absinthe, smoke, and talk until daybreak. I wasn't ready for camaraderie yet; I preferred solitude these days.

I threw open the door and hurried into my personal space. I stopped in my tracks and sucked in a breath. The room wasn't empty.

Moore.

My heart jumped into my throat as so many emotions bombarded me at once. I stared for a beat, making sure he was real. "How did you find me?"

"*Bonsoir, ma chérie.*"

His smug expression set my teeth on edge and instantly I realized my mistake, albeit three weeks too late. "My response to your newspaper advert. You had me tracked here. Damn it." I shut the door, closing us in together. "I don't want you here, Moore."

He rose out of the chair, straightening to his full height, and I looked him over, greedy for the little details I'd missed these last weeks. His suit was well-tailored, the expensive cloth designed to emphasize his power and strength. Lord, how I'd missed those shoulders and that broad chest. The strong jaw, the full lips that kissed me until I melted. Those threads of silver in his hair that I loved so much. My fingers itched with the need to touch him, to map every muscle and tendon once more.

Was he a bit thinner? I didn't remember his jacket hanging quite so loosely on him.

"You are far too talented for this abysmal show," was all he said.

Sighing, I tore my gaze off him and went to my dressing table. With my cream and a cloth, I began removing the heavy cosmetics from my face. "And you are far too high-handed. So you've found me. Congratulations."

"It wasn't easy. I don't know how you got out of the city without anyone noticing."

A wig and an Irish accent. I was an actress, after all. "Yet I did, which means I didn't wish to be found. But here you are."

"Did you think I would give up? I nearly tore the city apart in my search for you."

"And when that failed, you began placing adverts. The Fifth Avenue matrons must be horrified. No doubt they've run you out of town with pitchforks after such a public display for a woman so beneath you."

"You are not beneath me. And I don't care about what anyone says, not any longer."

"That's quite a change from two months ago."

"Rose," he said softly. "I love you. I think I've loved you since the very moment I saw you. When you walked out on the stage for the first time I felt a lightning bolt to my chest. I cannot live without you. These last two months have been the worst of my life."

Could this be true? I searched his face, looking for cracks in his story but finding none. "Worse than the divorce trial and the vitriol from the press?"

"A thousand times worse. I haven't been able to breathe or eat. I cannot stand to be apart from you. I'm so damn sorry I hurt you. Let me spend the rest of my life making it up to you."

Frowning, I threw the dirty cloth onto the dressing table. "We've been over this. I don't want to be your mistress."

"I don't want you as a mistress. I want you as a wife."

The earring I was removing slipped from my fingertips and dropped onto the table. Shock twisted my tongue into a knot. "A wife?" I managed. "You want to marry me."

"Yes."

Just like that? Was this how tycoons acquired their wives, by declaring it so? I didn't know whether to be hurt or insulted. Perhaps both.

I turned to face him, my voice sharp as I said, "Was that an attempt at a proposal of marriage?"

"No." Coming over to where I stood, he lowered himself to the floor, bending on one knee. "This is a proper proposal of marriage."

Oh. My heart began slamming inside my ribs, the force of my breathing picking up. Was he serious?

Moore produced a ring box and opened it. Nestled inside was a simple rose-cut diamond ring in a gold band. I covered my mouth with one hand, unable to take it all in. Moore grabbed my free hand and said, "Rose, I've never been happier than when we were together. You are the sun and the moon, the flowers and the trees. I'd rather face a thousand scandals than live without you. If you do me the great honor of becoming my wife, I promise to stand by your side proudly, publicly, as your partner, until the day I leave this earth."

I could feel tears building on my lashes, but he wasn't thinking rationally. "Moore, think about what you are doing. You'll never be accepted in polite society again. Your company—"

"None of that matters. None of it." He winced. "May I stand? I'm afraid my knees aren't what they once were."

Swallowing a teasing comment regarding his age, I helped him to his feet. "You say it doesn't matter now, but you will come to resent me when it's all stripped away."

"Sweetheart, nothing is being stripped. The board has been dealt with."

"What about your mother? She must hate the idea of an actress as a daughter-in-law."

"She wants me to be happy with whomever I choose. And she's eager for grandchildren, so I think that helps."

This was all sounding fantastical, like the end of an Austen novel. I pulled my hand from his and pinched the bridge of my nose. "This is madness. You must think about what you are asking before demanding an answer from me."

He tugged lightly on the pearls around my neck. "You're still wearing them."

I didn't want to tell him the truth, that I'd hardly taken them off since leaving New York. I could've sold the necklace in Paris and lived comfortably, but I wasn't able to bring myself to part with Moore's gift. "Moore, please. You must think about this, because you'll come to regret it."

"I've done nothing but think about this for the last two months. Ever since the morning you raised the idea, actually. I won't regret marrying you. I'll only regret not asking you sooner." He took my hand a second time. "Say yes, Rose. Let's be the two most scandalous people in New York together."

"What if I want to stay in Paris?"

"The Parisians are notoriously hard to shock, but I'm up for the challenge."

"Really?" I peered up at him. "You would stay here, if I wished?"

"Yes." He shook his head, like he was frustrated. "You're not listening. I'm keeping you, Rose, and to hell with what anyone has to say about it."

"You're serious. You really want to marry me."

"I truly, honestly, obsessively want to marry you." His eyes searched mine. "But what do you want? I'm older and you could do better than—"

"There's no one better." I moved closer, wrapping my arms around his neck. He was so solid and warm, and a sense of rightness settled into my veins. "Yes, I will marry you. Although I must warn you, I will shock New York Society by hosting the biggest, most lavish balls—between my work on the stage, of course."

He pulled me close and I heard him exhale a sigh of relief into my hair. "Thank god. I honestly didn't know how many additional adverts I could write."

"Tell me how you managed it. You knew I wouldn't be able to resist responding, didn't you?"

"Exactly." His hands moved to my waist and settled on my hips. "And once I knew you were in Paris, I paid Le Figaro to run my adverts every other day while I boarded a steamer bound for Europe."

I nuzzled his jaw. "I never thought you'd make your feelings widely known. You created a very public scandal to win me back."

"A worldwide scandal, actually. I didn't know where you were, so the first advert appeared in one hundred and twenty-six newspapers around the globe."

"You clever man," I whispered, shocked and pleased he'd gone to so much effort. "Are you going to kiss me now?"

"As soon as you put on my ring. I won't take advantage of you."

I laughed, but Moore didn't crack a smile. Warmth flooded my chest when I realized why. "This is because of what happened in Ohio."

Instead of answering, he took my hand and slipped the diamond ring on my finger. "There. Now you belong to me." He bent and placed a brief yet deep kiss on my mouth. "And I do hope that door locks because I'd very much like to take advantage of you."

I toyed with his collar stud. "What if I said that I preferred to wait until after we married?"

He didn't respond for a long moment, his body preternaturally still. "Then I suppose we would wait."

Grinning, I pulled him down for a kiss. "Good thing I would never say something so foolish. Hurry and lock the door, darling. I need you inside me."

Never in all my years had I seen a man move so fast . . .

* * *

**Thank you for reading *The Scandal of Rose*! You know I love a mistress story! ;-)**

**I'd love an honest review after you're finished, if you feel so inclined!**

**If you want a peek at what's next, keep reading!**

*A Peek at The Gilded Heiress*

**From USA Today bestselling author Joanna Shupe comes a spicy Anastasia story full of secrets and betrayal, set among the glittering streets of New York City's Gilded Age.**

In 1880 a baby was stolen from the wealthiest family in America. Though no ransom was ever demanded, the Pendelton family never gave up hope . . . and their reward became the stuff of legend.

After being raised in a children's asylum, Josie Smith ends up on the streets and quickly learns how to take care of herself. Her singing voice draws crowds on every corner, and she'll stop at nothing to become famous and travel the world, loved and adored by all. Maybe then she won't think about the family who gave her away as an infant.

Leo Hardy isn't afraid to use his charm and wits to make a fast buck, especially with a mother and five siblings to support. When he stumbles upon a beautiful young woman singing on the street, Leo notices her striking resemblance to the infamous missing baby's mother, Mrs. Thomas Pendelton. The Hardys lost everything thanks to the Pendeltons, and once Leo sees Josie, he seizes the opportunity to settle the score. All he needs to do is pull off the biggest swindle of his career.

As the two are catapulted into Knickerbocker High Society, they grow closer to their goal, as well as to each other. But secrets can only stay hidden for so long. Soon the truth unfolds, and both Josie and Leo must separate what's real from what's just gilding.

**Coming March 25, 2025 from HarperCollins Avon.**

**PREORDER HERE**

*Acknowledgments*

The last year has been a tough one for me, writing-wise. There just haven't been enough hours in the day. So, thank you for your patience when it comes to me putting more books out into the world.

Many hands help make these books shine. Thank you to Sabrina Darby for her editing and to Books and Moods for the gorgeous cover.

Thank you to Nicole Yost, the queen who keeps things running smoothly in my author life, allowing me to focus on writing. I'm very thankful for all she does, including brainstorming on this book!

Thank you also to Diana Quincy for her endless patience. And to my family, who truly deserve all the credit.

xox,

Joanna

Also by Joanna Shupe

**Fifth Avenue Rebels:**

The Heiress Hunt

The Lady Gets Lucky

The Bride Goes Rogue

The Duke Gets Even

**The Uptown Girls:**

The Rogue of Fifth Avenue

The Prince of Broadway

The Devil of Downtown

**The Four Hundred Series:**

A Daring Arrangement

A Scandalous Deal

A Notorious Vow

**The Knickerbocker Club:**

Tycoon

Magnate

Baron

Mogul

**Wicked Deceptions:**

The Courtesan Duchess

The Harlot Countess

The Lady Hellion

**Novellas:**

# About the Author

*USA Today* bestselling author **Joanna Shupe** has always loved history, ever since she saw her first Schoolhouse Rock cartoon. Since 2015, her books have appeared on numerous yearly "best of" lists, including *Publishers Weekly*, *The Washington Post*, *Kirkus Reviews*, Kobo, and BookPage.

Sign up for Joanna's Gilded Lilies Newsletter for book news, sneak peeks, reading recommendations, historical tidbits, and more!

Joanna also writes steamy contemporary mafia stories under the pen name **Mila Finelli**. If you're into that kind of thing, check out milafinelli.com.

www.joannashupe.com

www.ingramcontent.com/pod-product-compliance
Lightning Source LLC
Chambersburg PA
CBHW060459300726
48975CB00008B/2564